The Legend of the Inn at Maiden Falls...

There are lots of rumors, but no one is exactly sure why even the crankiest twosomes get so very coosome when they spend time at the historic Inn at Maiden Falls, nestled in the Colorado Rockies. Maybe it's the beautiful vista of all that rushing water (the falls) outside the windows. Maybe it's the clean, invigorating mountain air stirring up their blood. Or maybe (as the whispers say) there really are lusty ghosts of shady ladies past floating around the rafters. Old-timers say the inn was a famous brothel more than a hundred years ago; all the "soiled doves" may have mysteriously passed away, but their spirits remain to help young lovers discover the joy of sensual pleasure. Or so the story goes....

Dear Reader,

I'm thrilled to be part of Temptation's twentieth anniversary celebration! And I hope you're enjoying reading about Miss Arlotta and the girls in THE SPIRITS ARE WILLING miniseries as much as I've enjoyed working with fellow writers Julie Kistler and Colleen Collins. You probably already caught Colleen's book, *Sweet Talkin' Guy,* last month, and Julie Kistler's story, *It's in His Kiss,* will be on the shelves in August.

This July also marks the twentieth anniversary of the year Julie and I first met at a Romance Writers of America conference. So, to celebrate, we decided to come up with a project we could work on together. The idea behind THE SPIRITS ARE WILLING miniseries was inspired by Julie and Colleen's tour of a former brothel in Denver. Afterward I met them for a hilarious dinner in which we plotted the series and our characters.

Come visit with us in the community message boards at www.eHarlequin.com and stop by my Web site, www.HeatherMacAllister.com, for news about upcoming books.

Warmly,

Heather MacAllister

Books by Heather MacAllister

HARLEQUIN TEMPTATION
785—MOONLIGHTING
817—PERSONAL RELATIONS
864—TEMPTED IN TEXAS
892—SKIRTING THE ISSUE
928—MALE CALL
959—HOW TO BE THE PERFECT GIRLFRIEND

HEATHER MACALLISTER
CAN'T BUY ME LOVE

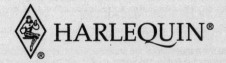

HARLEQUIN®

TORONTO • NEW YORK • LONDON
AMSTERDAM • PARIS • SYDNEY • HAMBURG
STOCKHOLM • ATHENS • TOKYO • MILAN • MADRID
PRAGUE • WARSAW • BUDAPEST • AUCKLAND

To Julie Kistler and Colleen Collins
Let's do this again sometime.

Special thanks to the New Braunfels group:
Christina Dodd, Connie Brockway, Susie Kay Law, Geralyn Dawson,
Susan Sizemore and our most excellent cook Bobbie Morganroth.
We should do that again sometime, too.

ISBN 0-373-69181-5

CAN'T BUY ME LOVE

Copyright © 2004 by Heather W. MacAllister.

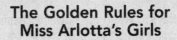

The Golden Rules for Miss Arlotta's Girls

We know rules are not your favorite things,
but some things need to be written down.
So here's your Golden Rules, girls. Abide by 'em
and we'll all do just fine. We weren't exactly angels
when we were here the first time around,
but we've got another chance. So we want to do what
we can to keep the idea of holy matrimony satisfying
so's nobody's man will be tempted to go lookin'
elsewhere for a good time. It may not seem fair,
but them's the rules. We helped 'em stray.
Now we're helping 'em stay.

Rule #1: You will never, ever do anything that might
come between the bride and groom.

Rule #2: No visibility. You can't be scarin'
the livin' daylights out of folks by fading in
and out or showing up in bits and pieces
at the wrong time.

Rule #3: Never, ever make love
with a guest yourself.
No exceptions.

Rule #4: No emotional attachments to
anyone. You can't follow them when they
leave, so you might as well not get attached.

Rule #5: When you have successfully put a troubled couple on the road to bedroom bliss, you earn a Notch in Miss Arlotta's Bedpost Book.

Rule #6: Especially good or bad activities may earn you Gold Stars or Black Marks.

Rule #7: It's gonna take ten Notches before you can advance. All Advancements shall be determined by Miss Arlotta and the Council, who will consider how difficult your couples were, how much work you had to do, your level of creativity, whether your heart was in the right place and those Gold Stars or Black Marks.

Rule #8: Any girl who disobeys these rules shall be punished.

Rule #9: Any and all rules may be changed by Miss Arlotta as she sees fit.

That's it. Push those couples into as much wedded bliss as they can handle, and we'll all do fine. You're all creative ladies when it comes to what happens between the sheets. So let's get to work and show 'em what kinds of sparks can fly when the spirits are willing!

Prologue

"I HAVE A REAL GOOD FEELING about today." Sunshine hitched herself onto the window seat in the bay window and retied the drawstring on her white bloomers. "It's a sunny day and I always have a good feeling about sunny days."

"You have a good feeling about every day. How you can be so cheerful and so dead at the same time is beyond my figuring. It's enough to drive a body, if I had a body, to drink. If I could drink." Flo drew her shawl more tightly around her shoulders.

Sunshine swung her foot and regarded Flo and the rest of the former good-time girls lounging in the parlor of what had once been one of the most exclusive bordellos in Colorado. "You're just cranky because your corset is too tight."

"I'm cranky because I'm dead! I'm dead and doomed to spend the rest of eternity in this corset because Mimi never came to loosen the knots."

Everyone looked at the dark-haired Mimi, dressed in a sumptuous French robe de chambre. She shrugged. "I, myself, was busy dying."

Over in the corner of a red-velvet chaise, Rosebud looked up from reading *Madame Bovary*. "Could we please talk about something else? We have discussed the fact that we're dead every day for the past one hundred and nine years. There was a gas leak. We died. It's time to move on."

"I would love to move on!" Flo shifted uncomfortably. "I can't believe that Belle Bulette, of all people, has gone to the Great Sunday Picnic in the Sky and I'm still here."

"I miss Belle," Sunshine said wistfully. But she smiled as she said it.

"You would."

"It was never this boring when she was around," said another one of the girls, a strawberry blonde in a lavender chemise.

"Oh, I know. She was always so spirited."

"Spirited—ha, ha."

"Oh, Flo, you know what I meant."

"One makes one's own excitement and profits, as vell. Is zat not so?" An elegant woman dressed in a Chinese-silk wrapper lounged against the doorway next to one of the brass-potted palms. She gestured toward the guests checking into what was now the Inn at Maiden Falls. "Specifically, I vould like to make some excitement viz zat fine young buck."

"Countess, you know the rules," Sunshine reminded her.

"My dear, for him, I vould break zee rules."

Sunshine watched as a lone male—they all had such broad shoulders these days—checked into the hotel. He had a fine face, sure enough, and held himself with a confidence that promised confidence in the bedroom, as well.

However, everyone knew Miss Arlotta's Golden Rules, specifically the no hanky-panky rule, and what would happen if a girl broke them—a black mark in the Bedpost Book. Too many black marks and there would never be a chance of earning the ten notches it took to go to the Eternal Picnic.

After decades of bemoaning their fate, Miss Arlotta and Judge Hangen, who had unfortunately been visiting Miss Arlotta at the time of the gas leak, figured out that since they'd sold fake love in life, they could redeem themselves by selling true love in death.

Or something. Whatever the reasoning, their plan seemed to be working.

Sunshine didn't know if there was exactly a Great Picnic, or an Eternal Picnic, or whatever, but when they were alive, every Sunday Miss Arlotta's boarders had dressed in their finest and driven the buggy through the town of Maiden Falls to the lovely shaded meadow where they'd picnicked and laughed and sometimes taken a dip in the pool beneath the falls.

Sunshine and the others had loved the Sunday picnics—even Belle, the sharpshooting, whiskey-drinking cynical gambler. It had taken quite a lot of man to handle Belle. And quite a lot of men had.

Anyway, being outside, feeling the grass tickle her bare feet, wading in the pool, even just plain lying around in the shade was what Sunshine missed the most.

She and the others couldn't leave the inn proper. Oh, they could go out on the roof, but it wasn't the same.

But what if they didn't even have that? It could be worse. And now they knew that there was a way to go on to—if not the Great Picnic as they'd taken to calling it—then someplace else fine and good. Someplace Belle had gone. Someplace Sunshine was going to go, too, as soon as she helped one more couple on the path to true love. So fine, face or no, the man wasn't worth risking a black mark.

"Ooh-la-la. That is a fine one indeed." Mimi's accent became more pronounced the nearer a man got to her. It was generally agreed that she more than likely came from Paris, Texas, rather than Paris, France.

"He must be the groom." Sunshine, along with the others, drifted over to the lobby check-in desk. "There's a wedding this weekend, you know." She clasped her hands together. "I just love weddings."

"Oh, that was canceled," Lavender said.

"It's back on," Rosebud informed them from her place on the chaise. She was more interested in her book, which Lord knows she'd had over a hundred years to read, than she was in men. She simply didn't know any better. Poor Rosebud had the misfortune of arriving at Miss Arlotta's just before the gas leak, so her experience of men was extremely limited. Extremely.

"If the wedding is back on, then the bride and groom must need help," Sunshine said.

"Same wedding, different bride and groom," Rosebud told her.

"Me, I would like to give that man some very special help."

Lavender sighed. "Oh, Mimi, wouldn't we all."

"I wouldn't," Flo snapped. "No man is worth giving up the chance of a loosened corset."

"Amen to that," drawled a voice from the door of

the secret passage. "Listen up, ladies, and Glory Hallelujah will set you straight. Desdemoaner and I have been on the roof and, y'all, that man is not the groom. Looky yonder at the door."

At that moment, a distinguished older man with silver temples and a full head of salt-and-pepper hair strode through the lobby as though he owned the place.

Sunshine had seen his type before—usually with a gavel in his hand or a badge on his chest.

"Behold, the groom."

"Oh, it's an older couple then. A second marriage maybe? How nice." Sunshine ignored all the eye rolling. So she chose to look on the bright side all the time. Might as well enjoy life, er, death. Or whatever limbo they were in.

"Not quite." Glory hooked her thumb over her shoulder as a dark-suited younger woman joined the man at the reception desk.

She had her hair cut in one of those styles that looked as though she'd hacked at it with a dull knife on a windy day. Sunshine patted her own long curls.

"His daughter?" Flo asked.

"The bride," Glory announced.

"And I say brava!" The Countess clapped slowly.

"And, me, I say it depends on how much money he has." Mimi rubbed her fingers together.

Flo cackled. "Honey, it wouldn't take much for me."

"It never did, Flo, it never did," the Countess murmured.

"I heard that!"

"And so did I." A voice boomed around them.

Sunshine could never figure out how Miss Arlotta, who spent most of her time in the attic, was nevertheless able to hear all and see all and speak to them wherever they were.

"Sunshine! The bride is checking into your room." Lavender was hovering behind the guest register.

"And the groom?" Mimi asked.

"The new section."

"Well, that can't be good," Glory said.

"Why not? You know the groom isn't supposed to see the bride on their wedding day until she walks down the aisle." Sunshine sighed. "It's so romantic."

"Sunshine will assist this couple," Miss Arlotta pronounced. "Older gentlemen are her speciality."

"Thank you, Miss Arlotta!" Sunshine drew a deep breath as the others protested—but not too much—before gradually drifting away to other parts of the inn. Older men who were lonely and liked her youthful looks and innocent chatter had been, indeed, her speciality.

She felt a tug on her gauzy wrapper. Rosebud had abandoned her book and was watching the couple check in. "You can drop the act," she murmured. "We're alone."

"What act?" Sunshine batted her eyelashes.

"They have blonde jokes now, you know."

"I beg your pardon?"

"Jokes about girls with yellow hair being dumb." She tweaked one of Sunshine's sausage curls. "Only you're not dumb."

Sunshine kept her smile in place. "And don't you forget it, sweetie."

"I mean...take all this romantic talk. This was a place of business."

Sunshine laughed. "Sure was—monkey business."

"It was sex for money." Rosebud pushed her wire-rim glasses up higher on her nose. "The men gave us money and we gave them sex. It was as simple as that."

Sunshine looked across the lobby at the couple. Other than briefly resting his hand on the small of the woman's back, the man never touched her. And she didn't touch him. They smiled politely instead of the wide, tooth-baring grins of people who can't help smiling. Of people who are in love.

"Rosebud," she murmured, "it was never as simple as that."

1

WHEN ALEXIS O'HARA ARRIVED at the Inn at Maiden Falls, Colorado, for her wedding and encountered an ex-boyfriend also checking in, she gave him a cool I'm-looking-good-and-aren't-you-sorry-you-dumped-me smile. When he informed her he was representing her fiancé in the pre-nup negotiations, she did what any successful, independent, modern woman did when faced with the unthinkable: she called her mother.

Abandoning her luggage in the center of a lovely Aubusson rug as soon as she got to her room, Alexis stared unseeingly out the window at the gorgeous Rocky Mountain vista, cell phone pressed to her ear. "Mom?"

"You've changed your mind," Patty O'Hara said flatly.

"No! Why do you keep assuming that every time I call?"

"Oh, I don't know—maybe the week-long engagement to a man I've never before heard you mention in a romantic context?"

"This isn't that sort of marriage."

"What sort of marriage is it?"

Alexis began to speak, fully intending to extol the virtues of compatibility, admiration and shared interests, but heard herself say, "It's an I'm-tired-of-dating marriage."

"Oh, one of those. I thought it was an old-fashioned marry-an-old-guy-for-his-money marriage."

Alexis gritted her teeth, then craftily pointed out, "He's fifty-four. That's only two years younger than you. Are you saying you're old?"

"I'm saying I've been married to a fifty-four-year-old man and I know what it's like."

She was talking about Alexis's father. Alexis preferred not to think of her father in that context. "But you haven't been married to a *rich* fifty-four-year-old man."

There was silence.

"Mom?"

"I was giving you time to think. You've been rushing around like a madwoman and I know you haven't fully considered what you're doing."

"I had plenty of time to think on the plane." Actually, she'd fallen asleep on the plane. Missed the honey peanuts and everything. "I'm not changing my mind."

"I'm still not cutting the tags off my dress until I have to walk to my seat."

"Mom." Alexis pressed the area between her eyebrows.

"Alexis, as with any mother, I just want you to be happy. Now, I know you didn't call to argue and I'm in the middle of packing. What's up?"

"Dylan's here." Alexis was proud that her voice sounded calm and matter-of-fact.

"Do I know her?"

"*Him.*"

"Well, you never know these days with one-size-fits-all names."

"Like Pat?" Alexis asked dryly, although no one ever called her mother Pat.

"A nickname for Patricia. What's Dylan a nickname for?"

Alexis exhaled. "Trouble."

"Why?"

How could her mother have forgotten? "Law school? The guy who drop-kicked my heart into orbit around Planet Pity?"

"Oh. That Dylan."

"Yes, that Dylan! How could you forget that Dylan?"

"There've been...so many..."

Yes, her heart had made many trips to Planet Pity since then. But it had orbited longer over Dylan than anyone else. "Mom, he's negotiating the pre-nup for Vincent."

"You be careful with that pre-nup. Don't sign anything without reading it first."

"Mom! I'm a lawyer, too! You're missing the point. *Dylan* is representing my *fiancé*."

"Do you still have feelings for him?" her mother asked carefully.

"Yes—hate!"

"I thought you were over him."

"I...am." The unguarded rush of pleasure she'd experienced when she'd seen him in the lobby was just a holdover from their school years. "And I don't hate him. I haven't thought of him." Much. "But he's going to be negotiating my pre-nup with Vincent!"

"He apparently doesn't feel that it'll be a conflict of interest."

"That's because he's not interested. Forget I said that." This conversation was not going well.

"So...what do you want from me?" asked her mother.

"Tell me what to do!"

"Wait...Alexis asks her mother for advice. Let me go write this date on the calendar."

Alexis rolled her eyes. "Maybe if you weren't so sarcastic, I might ask your advice more often."

"No, you wouldn't."

"You're probably right. But I am asking now." Her mother was an investment banker. Analyzing was her forte.

"Let's take a couple of steps back and look at the big picture. What do you want? And that's not a cop-out."

"I want him not to be here."

"Because of Vincent or because of him?"

"Because it's awkward."

"If Dylan were female, would it be as awkward?"

"Yeeeees," Alexis said slowly. "If I were close friends with a woman and we broke off our friendship, I would feel awkward having her as my fiancé's counsel. Yes," she said more firmly. "It's that kind of awkwardness."

"Hmm. If Dylan were female, would you ask Vincent to find other representation?"

Alexis skirted the question. "It's too late now."

"Isn't Denver close by? Surely there are other lawyers available. But the point here is that you'd probably mention it to Vincent if Dylan were female. So why not tell him how uncomfortable you feel anyway? You're marrying the man. You should be able to talk about such things with him."

"Because...because..." Because she just wanted to marry Vincent and get it over with. "I don't want Dylan to know he makes me uncomfortable."

"Or you don't want to chance Vincent discovering that you once had a relationship with his lawyer?" Her mother had found the core of the problem, as Alexis had known she would.

"That sounds so much worse than it is. Truly, this is no big deal and I don't want it to become a big deal. But if I don't mention it and Vincent already knows or finds out, then he'll think I'm hiding something. If I do make a point of telling him about Dylan and me, then I'm drawing unnecessary attention to it, especially if he didn't already know. And I don't know if Dylan has told him or not. And I can't ask Dylan because then he'll think I care whether or not Vincent knows and then Dylan will think he has something over me. A bargaining chip maybe. Which is stupid because whether or not I was once in love with him is not important. But Vincent might think it is." She stopped and drew a deep breath. "My head hurts."

"Poor baby."

"Oh, Mom. What'll I do?"

"Okay. I suggest you treat Dylan the way you'd treat any other former classmate, male or female. You smile, make casual chitchat, go over your pre-nup and send him on his way."

Smile. Chitchat. Pre-nup. Dylan leaves. Okay. She could do that. "But what if he says something?"

"If he actually has the poor taste to bring up your past personal relationship in front of the man who is his client and your fiancé, you smile, casually acknowledge it, express regret that you've lost track of each other and that you don't have more time to catch up now, then leave."

Casual. Leave. This could work. She especially liked the leaving scenarios. "Thanks, Mom."

"Alexis?"

"Yeah?"

"A shot of tequila afterward wouldn't hurt."

"AND ON THE FIRST ANNIVERSARY of the marriage ceremony, if no petition for dissolution has been filed, Alexis O'Hara shall be entitled to receive from the Individual Property of Vincent Cathardy, the sum of one hundred thousand dollars plus the salary she would expect to earn if she is not employed. Said salary will be computed according to the formulas in attachment A. On the second anniversary of the marriage ceremony, if no petition for dissolution has been filed, Ms. O'Hara shall be entitled to receive from the Individual Property of Vincent Cathardy, the sum of two hundred thousand dollars plus the salary she would expect to earn if she is not employed. On the third anniversary..."

And so on and so on. It was a humdinger of a prenup, but then Dylan Greene had always thought Alexis O'Hara was a humdinger of a woman.

Not that he'd had any recent firsthand experience of her humdingerness, but if memory served...

However, memory shouldn't be serving anything right now. Dylan should concentrate on the clauses he was reading. Alexis and her lawyer would be. Vincent would be, too, though he'd written most of the contract himself. Go figure.

Dylan needed to remain sharp. Yeah, he was good and had a reputation as the go-to guy in family law and, if pressed, would admit that the reputation was deserved. After all, he'd successfully faced-off against big-shot lawyer Vincent in a number of pre-nup cases. All things considered, he'd been flattered, enormously flattered—all right, make that totally stunned—when Vincent Cathardy had retained him to negotiate the prenuptial agreement prior to the man's own forthcoming marriage.

Vincent, senior partner in Swinehart, Cathardy and Steele, was a legend. His name was spoken in hushed tones. A lawyer going up against Vincent Cathardy could expect to receive at least half-a-dozen bottles of sympathy Scotch. Since Vincent Cathardy was a corporate lawyer and Dylan's firm specialized in family law, Vincent wasn't a regular opponent. When he was, the case usually involved family businesses and disputed inheritances or, of course, divorces. High-profile divorces. Expensive divorces.

Dylan wasn't much of a drinker and he thought he probably had maybe four bottles left from the last time he'd faced Vincent Cathardy. Anyway, he kept waiting to discover the catch. He and Vincent didn't move in the same legal—or social—circles. So why had Vincent hired him?

And then he'd caught the name of the bride on the papers. Alexis O'Hara. Alexis. Brilliant and ambitious Alexis.

She was working on a pretty good legend, herself, being Vincent's right-hand man, or woman, as it were. Had she suggested Dylan? Nah. Not judging by the pinched look on her face when she'd walked into the lobby.

He hadn't prepared himself for his first sight of her because he didn't think he needed to. He'd been wrong, as his body quickly informed him. His heart had kicked up a notch—several notches—his blood had warmed and things had definitely stirred in the southern regions. Just like that. Seven years since he'd seen her and just like that his every nerve was attuned to her. He'd barely stopped himself from sweeping her into his arms and kissing her with a pent-up passion that would have left no doubt as to their former relationship. But he had stopped himself and returned Alexis's cool, polite smile with one of his own.

Vincent had been standing there, of course, and Vincent was the sort of man who would have made it his business to learn that Dylan and Alexis were once involved. But that was law school, Dylan reminded himself. Puppy love. Over long ago. A fond memory, very fond as his reaction just told him, but nothing more. Certainly no threat to the big guy.

No, the reason Vincent had hired him was more likely Dylan's record when they'd gone head-to-head.

That must be it. The man respected him. Figured he was one of the best.

He was, but men of Vincent's stature and experience wouldn't like to admit it. And choosing Dylan to negotiate his pre-nup? Vincent had to know he was elevating Dylan to the legal stratosphere. But if he thought that entitled him to any special legal wrangling, then he thought wrong.

Dylan continued to read, conscious of the utter silence in the room except for the sound of his voice. No objections so far. And why would Alexis object? She was going to get her salary and a bonus for each year she stayed married to the guy. And it was payable during the marriage, not a settlement upon dissolution of the marriage. No, Alexis would be getting a nice little anniversary present each year. The funds were to become her separate property. Nice work, if you could get it, and Alexis apparently could.

He hadn't figured her for the type, the give-it-all-up and-lounge-around-the-pool-between-spa-treatments type. Not before her legal brilliance had a chance to shine on its own.

What a waste.

But his opinion was completely inappropriate. He wasn't supposed to be having opinions.

And he wasn't supposed to be thinking about Alexis. Seeing her again had an unnerving effect on him. It was as though he'd entered a classroom to find her waiting for him as usual, and he was entitled to the hot feelings that coursed through him. But he wasn't entitled. Unfortunately, the feelings were still coursing. He was remembering long hours spent in her arms, kissing until their lips had gone numb, studying until they'd fallen asleep together. The scent of her skin and hair. The curve at her waist. The—no. *Put the memories away, Dylan.*

Alexis had become a striking woman, not that he'd expected her to go to seed or anything. He was going to have to watch himself this weekend.

Dylan glanced up to find her inky-black gaze on him. He'd always been fascinated by her eyes. They were the darkest brown he'd ever seen. It was unnerving to stare at them, and she knew it and used her eyes to excellent advantage.

Once or twice, he'd seen emotion in those eyes, but not often. And not now.

DYLAN STILL HADN'T DEVELOPED a poker face, Alexis saw. He'd always been easy to read, so when he'd split up with her without warning a few weeks before graduation, she'd been stunned that she'd never seen it coming. Even now, she could remember the expression in his eyes. Surprise that she was so upset. And pity—she'd hated that.

But no regret. No second thoughts.

Now, those warm, caramel-colored emotional semaphores were signaling disapproval across the polished walnut of the Victorian dining table.

As if he had any right to approve or disapprove of anything she did.

And so what if he or anyone else did disapprove? If Alexis wanted to marry Vincent, then that's what she was going to do. She'd earned the right to do whatever she wanted. She'd worked hard for years, and guess what? She'd been working to achieve a certain kind of life and now that she was pulling in the kind of money to support that life, she didn't have the time or the energy to enjoy it.

Alexis was tired of working at this insane pace. And darn it, she wanted kids eventually, but she didn't want to be put on the mommy track because she couldn't routinely work eighty to ninety hours a week or because she took off a couple of years.

That's what had happened to every woman who'd given birth while Alexis had been at Swinehart, Cathardy and Steele. And it wasn't just her firm, or even law, itself. Even Marisa, who'd joined the firm at the same time as Alexis, and who had her mother, younger sister *and* a nanny living with her, had given up and now consulted from her home.

So, it still came down to family or career. But why did women have to make this wrenching choice? Why couldn't they do both? She'd never heard of the men in her office agonizing over it. She knew they had families. New photos of smiling wives and children regularly sprouted on their desks, although that could be so they could recognize them when they crossed paths at home.

Still, they had something she didn't. Something she wanted. And by marrying Vincent, she could have it. She could have it all.

A week ago, she'd been looking forward to collapsing and sleeping late Saturday morning—maybe even sleeping the whole weekend. She so rarely had a weekend off. She'd just given herself the old pep talk, the one that said being primary associate on Vincent's high-profile team was worth it. Worth no personal life, worth the lack of sleep, worth missing birthdays and holidays, worth never really getting to know her three-year-old niece.

She could slow down later, she'd always assured herself at the end. That was the point when she usually slipped into her fantasy, the one filled with shopping, salon appointments, lunches and sleep, glorious sleep.

Except, she wanted to slow down—stop—now. She wanted the fantasy now. She hadn't felt the same sense of satisfaction that she used to feel at the end of a big project. And the oblique remarks made by her mother and sister now stung. She would never know her three-year-old niece, her sister, Leigh, pointed out, because she hadn't seen her niece as a three year old. And unless Alexis managed a trip to Austin before May 24, Madison's fourth birthday, she wouldn't.

Alexis had checked her Palm and found out that Leigh was right.

It had given her something to think about.

She'd been thinking about it last Friday after she and Vincent had finished work on a huge merger. Vincent had opened a bottle of champagne and the two crystal flutes she'd drunk coupled with the feeling of accomplishment and the magnificent high-rise view from Vincent's equally magnificent office had loosened her tongue.

Vincent had waved an arm at the lights of Houston winking at them and asked, "How does it feel to look out there and know you're one of the best?"
She'd answered, "Not the way I thought it would."

"Then you need more champagne," Vincent had said. That was when he'd poured the fateful second flute.

Alexis never drank more than one drink in a business setting. But, Vincent was her mentor and she was so used to following his advice that she'd held out her flute without a second thought.

He'd clinked their glasses together and then she'd rashly drained hers, never tasting the pricey Dom something or other that Vincent kept chilled in his office refrigerator.

"Well?" One thick eyebrow raised. His face was impossibly tanned. Impossibly as in, where did he find the time to have the fake tan sprayed on? Alexis hadn't even managed to find a reliable manicurist to come to her office.

"How do you feel now?" Vincent had asked.

"I want more," she remembered saying. But when he'd held up the bottle, she'd shaken her head. "Not champagne. *More.*"

A smile had curved his lips.

Now that she thought about it, Alexis recalled that it was the same smile he gave opponents before obliterating them. It was an I've-won-but-I'm-going-to-play-with-you-awhile smile.

She hadn't been an opponent, had she?

"You're entitled to more." He'd named a figure.

To her astonishment, Alexis had realized she'd negotiated a raise without even trying. "Has all this been worth it to you?" she'd asked him.

He'd looked her right in the eyes, his blue ones so

bright and so sharp they cut through her champagne haze. "Absolutely."

Alexis had felt herself relax until he added, "But then my biological clock runs longer than yours."

Biological clock. Hadn't that become a cliché yet? And yet once he'd mentioned it, she'd realized all her unease was probably related to that same biological clock. Cliché or not, she was thirty-one and had no boyfriend and no time to find one, along with tattered friendships and blood relatives who were strangers. She'd poured out all this to an uncharacteristically sympathetic Vincent. Oh, it had been a calculated sympathy, Alexis knew that, but she'd pretended she didn't.

And then he'd said, "I have a proposal for you." And that's exactly what it had been.

She'd been shocked and then the idea had grown on her. Though he was older, Vincent was by no means unattractive and quite frankly, he could provide a better life for her than she could provide for herself.

And she didn't want to hear any of this letting-down-the-sisterhood stuff, either. She'd just like to see how many of the sisterhood would turn down an offer like the one Vincent had made. Not many, and not Alexis.

So here she was, a week later, marrying a man she admired, but didn't love. Who admired, but didn't love, her. Still, they both wanted the same thing—a family and children. Well, Alexis also wanted a personal trainer and a standing appointment with a masseuse, but basically, she and Vincent were on the same page.

It made so much sense—Alexis would settle into the marriage for a couple of months, then work on having children right away, and by the time they were well into elementary school, Vincent would be ready to take over parenting duties and Alexis would pick up her legal career where she left off. Thanks to Vincent, there would be no mommy track for Alexis. As one of the founding partners, he had that kind of power, and he was putting it in writing, right in this pre-nup that she should be paying attention to instead of mentally justifying her actions to a pair of caramel-colored eyes that still had the power to affect her.

"Alexis?" Margaret, her lawyer, gave her a look that meant Alexis had missed something.

In her late forties, Margaret had never married. She was hard as nails, humorless, and her roots needed re-touching.

She was Alexis's future.

No, not anymore. Not now that she was marrying Vincent. "Margaret?"

"Do you agree to the terms of the preceding clause?"

"I…"

"There is a significant—" Margaret paused to emphasize just how significant "—monetary penalty should you return to work. In addition, there is a non-compete clause that troubles me."

"It didn't trouble Alexis," Vincent inserted smoothly.

"We have had barely forty-eight hours to review the contract." Margaret peered at Vincent over the top of some unflattering reading glasses. They were in no way stylish, nor had they ever been. Shopping for frames would take time, time a high-powered attorney like Margaret didn't have.

"I would suggest that if Alexis works for another firm, you mitigate the financial penalty," she said.

"I wouldn't work for another firm." That would be defeating the whole purpose of the marriage.

Margaret and her awful glasses turned to Alexis. "All the more reason to take a second look at those financial terms."

Alexis didn't want to take a second look. Truly, she was going to start on a family right away and planned to spend the next few years decorating nurseries and changing diapers in between rejuvenating facials. No sense in wasting time. No sense in destroying the lovely weightless bubbly feeling she'd had ever since she'd agreed to marry Vincent and let him worry about acquiring money for a while.

And then Dylan spoke. "Vincent, I usually advise my clients to provide for the unexpected. In this instance, a clause dealing with your possible incapacitation would not be amiss. Should your income stop, under these terms, Alexis would be penalized for supporting you."

Dylan sure was a real lead weight.

Vincent gave him a patronizing smile. "If I had wanted such a clause, then I would have inserted it myself."

"If you'd thought of it."

"I did."

"Judges like to see those clauses." Dylan wasn't intimidated in the slightest, Alexis would give him that, though not much more. "They're a sign of good faith and make the pre-nup harder to break."

"I expect an unbreakable contract from you, Dylan. Is my faith misplaced?"

"Not if your faith takes my advice."

Sheesh. Why didn't they just unzip their pants and get out rulers?

"Alexis has faith, don't you, Alexis?" Vincent asked.

Dylan's gaze flicked to Alexis at the same time Margaret's foot nudged hers. Yeah, yeah. The clause should be there. She couldn't help feeling that it was some kind of test, though.

"Vincent..." she began.

"If I'm incapacitated, then more than ever, I would want my lovely wife by my side." He reached across the table and squeezed Alexis's hand. "We'd hardly be destitute. I have a lifetime income from the firm."

"Oh." Wow. Maybe she'd never go back to work. Work was overrated. Spa paraffin and sea-salt scrub pedicures were not. Alexis slipped back into her fantasy as one of the rich and idle.

She heard a buzz and saw Vincent remove his cell phone. "Excuse me. I need to take this." He raised his eyebrows at Alexis. "Briarwood."

The next big case. One that she would have been working on with him if she hadn't been planning a wedding in a week. "Of course," she mouthed. But Vincent had already turned away and was leaving the room.

"Alexis, you and I need to talk."

"Margaret—"

"But not now." Margaret picked up her copy of the contract and stood. "I'm going to look up a couple of things." She pointed at Dylan. "You know the rules. No discussing the contract unless I'm present."

Dylan sat back in the chair, palms outward. "Hey. She's a lawyer, too."

"She *was*," Margaret stated over her shoulder as she jogged out the doorway.

That stung a little until Alexis told herself that Margaret was just jealous. Who wouldn't be?

She turned her gaze to the man across the table to find him watching her. She watched him back. He looked the same. More polished and with shorter hair, but basically the same. They might have been sitting across from each other at one of the heavy wooden library tables at school. They'd always had to put the table between them so they could concentrate on studying instead of each other.

It rarely worked then and it wasn't working now.

Dylan had never been one of those catch-your-breath attractive men, but he made the effort with what he had and the effect was a nonthreatening handsomeness. Except now, it was threatening her peace of mind. She narrowed her eyes at his tan. Fake. When did these men have the time?

"So," he said.

"So," she said back. He was going to be trouble. She could tell already.

"Long time no see."

"Commencement." She'd stared at the back of his head two rows ahead and alternated between fury and heartbreak. But she'd recovered.

"So how have you been, Alexis?"

"Good. I've kept busy."

"You're being overly modest. The mere mention of your name strikes fear into the hearts of small-business owners everywhere."

Was that a compliment, or not? And did she care? "I've heard your name bandied about, as well."

"I'll bet you have."

"Usually 'that damn Dylan Greene.' You should change your letterhead to D. Dylan Greene."

He laughed. "Yeah. Vincent has had to restructure a couple of deals when he couldn't break one of my pre-nups."

"Actually, I did the restructuring." Hours and hours and hours of restructuring.

"You get to do the dirty work, huh?"

Alexis folded her hands on the table in front of her. Gripped her knuckles, actually. Hard. "I get the experience."

"Which you are now throwing away."

Alexis drew a deep breath. So much for their stilted little conversation. "Watch it, Dylan."

"I am watching it." He pushed back from the table and stood. Shoving his hands in his pockets he walked over to the huge windows looking out on the Colorado mountains. "I'm watching a woman throw away her career. What happened to you, Alexis?"

2

ALEXIS WAS INSTANTLY ANGRY on so many levels, she could barely respond. "Are you married, Dylan?"

"No."

"Been married?"

"No."

"Given birth?"

He leveled a look at her.

"Anyone given birth on your behalf?"

"Not that I am aware of."

"So you really don't know what's at stake for women who have children? Things are very different for men and women."

"No duh."

"Ooh. Like the technical lawyer-speak, Dylan."

"I'm not speaking as a lawyer. It's against the rules."

"Then what are you speaking as?"

"A friend."

"I think not." She'd been aiming for matter-of-fact, but had hit snippy.

He smiled. No grinned, damn it. "You're still mad at me."

"I am so over you." She was. She *was*.

"You're still mad. Yes, you are." The grin widened. "I must be a better lover than I thought."

Typical. "I've had worse," she told him. "And I've had better. You're somewhere in the middle. Average." Honestly, never tell a man he was the worst lover you ever had, he wouldn't believe it. But mediocre? Now that really got to him.

"And how does Vincent rank?"

She couldn't believe he'd asked that. "You're not the first to imply that Vincent must have selected me to be on his team because I slept with him, but you're the most unexpected. That was unworthy of you, Dylan."

He blinked. "I wasn't impugning your legal skill." Watching her carefully, he continued softly, "You're marrying the guy."

"Yes."

"So it's a safe assumption you've slept with him."

They stared at each other and Alexis knew that she must not look away. Didn't dare blink. She was good at this game. Her eyes were so dark people remarked on them. She used cosmetics to emphasize them and she practiced chilling expressions that revealed nothing.

However, eyes were one thing. The blush she was horrified to feel creeping up her throat was something else. She, who could bluff anyone, could not bluff Dylan.

She blinked.

And he pounced. "You've never slept with the guy."

Alexis darted a look toward the doorway. How mortifying if Vincent or Margaret caught them discussing such a subject. "That—is—none—of—your—business."

Dylan sat on the edge of the table. "But I'm fascinated by your logic—or the lack thereof. What the heck are you doing, Alexis?"

"I'm thinking with my head and not with my heart. 'If more people thought with their heads instead of their hearts, we'd be out of a job.' You said that."

"I did. Go on."

"Well," she deliberately lowered her voice, injecting a sultry quality, "you know that first, wonderful rush of passion, when two people can't get enough of each other, when they're blind to anything else about each other as long as they can be entwined for hours and hours...?"

His eyes had darkened. Alexis thought he might even be drooling. He nodded and swallowed.

Deliberately breaking the mood, she sat back and threw up her hands. "It never lasts. And then you're stuck with what's left. And you look around and think, 'Ick. I can't live with that. What was I thinking?' And then you realize you weren't thinking. You were seduced by the sizzle. This time, I evaluated the rest of the man first. And he's some man." She gave Dylan her best seductive smile. "I'll fire up the sizzle later. And you know I can."

For a moment, she would have sworn that she had him, then he said, "Better make sure you've got some good wood."

"Don't be crude."

"Hey, I'm just saying that if you want little sizzlers,

you're going to have to build the campfire with something."

"And explain to me why you care about my campfire?"

He reached toward her and she thought he was going to touch her. She just stopped herself from flinching as he tapped the contract before her. "I want to know if successful career women selling themselves as high-priced wives is the new trend."

"You're being deliberately insulting."

He eyed her speculatively. "I might be trying to shake you up and see if all your cylinders are firing."

"Do you ever use plain English?"

"I thought the statement about selling yourself as a high-priced wife was pretty plain."

"I look on it as protecting my future and the future of my children."

"I'm listening."

He was. And Alexis wanted to explain. "I want children and the thing is, a woman risks a lot careerwise these days. As soon as she's visibly pregnant, she loses her edge. If she becomes angry, it's hormones. Sad? Hormones. Aggressive? Hormones. So it's 'let's not put too much pressure on the little mother.' Give her the routine cases. Don't let her start long-term litigation, because she'll be taking maternity leave. And from then on, she's on the mommy track, because she can't work the long hours she has been because children get sick and she'll have child-care problems. And guilt. Let's not forget the guilt. I have seen it happen over and over again. For some reason, men don't have these problems. He takes time off to meet with the kid's teacher and he's a caring and involved father. She takes time off and she's allowing her children to interfere with her work. I don't want to have to choose between my children and my career, so I'll take time off in the beginning and go back to work when they're older. The beauty of it is that I'll pick up right where I left off. That's what it says in the contract. My lovely, lovely contract. So don't talk to me about throwing away my career. I'm preserving it."

Dylan regarded her for a moment, then moved closer on the table until he was sitting right next to her, and then he stared at her some more.

She didn't want him staring at her and she didn't want him sitting next to her. He was too close. He made her too aware of him as a man, a man that, in spite of herself, she still wanted. After all this time, it wasn't fair that her body would betray her this way.

Alexis looked down at her copy of the prenuptial agreement, flinching when Dylan nudged her chin upward with his knuckles. "You're not in love with him."

"How could you possibly know how I feel?"

His voice deepened. "Because I remember how you look when you think you're in love."

What a low blow. She had been in love. She'd thought Dylan was The One. "Someone once told me that there're all kinds of love and not all of them come with a ring. This time, I get the ring."

YEAH, HE'D SAID THAT, TOO. Had actually used it again, it was such a good line. But she was missing the point.

Dylan indicated the contract. "That's not a ring. It's a noose."

"I'm well aware of your feelings on marriage."

He gave a huge mock sigh. "Alexis, Alexis, Alexis."

"What?"

"This isn't the same. Back then, we'd both worked very hard. And we were going to be working very hard. In different cities. Remember? You were staying in Austin and I was going to Houston." An awful thought occurred to him. "You didn't go with the Swinehart firm because it's in—"

"Of course not." She spoke with ego-deflating scorn.

"Marriage was impossible then. Neither of us was ready—" *he* hadn't been ready "—and I figured you knew it. But you got serious all of a sudden." Maybe he'd been naive, but he'd thought they could keep in touch as they began their careers. After all, it was what they'd worked for. What they'd talked about. What they'd wanted. Serious life commitments could come later.

"It wasn't all of a sudden," she snapped. "I was expecting something entirely different that afternoon. I thought you were going to propose."

He'd long suspected as much. "I'm sorry. Truly I am. But if we'd stayed together then, we wouldn't be together now. Not with both of us having the kind of careers we've had."

She didn't say anything and it irked him. "Marriage would have held you back. You know it's true. Come on. Admit it."

"Maybe it would have held *you* back."

He just shook his head.

Crossing her arms over her chest, Alexis looked to the side. "You're right. Happy now?"

He wasn't. He wasn't at all. Not because of the wrong timing for the two of them, but because his conscience was telling him she was making a big mistake now and he should stop her. Funny, he never remembered his conscience being this loud before. However, it still made a valid point. Marriage to him wasn't right for her then, and marriage to Vincent wasn't right for her now.

"Anyway, every relationship I've had since has fallen apart. So instead of basing a relationship solely on mutual attraction and hoping that everything else works out, Vincent and I are basing our marriage on affection, compatibility, respect and shared goals and interests. If we find passion, great. But passion fades. At least I know we've got something solid left."

"Yeah. Over a hundred thousand solids each year."

She gave him that blank look she was so good at. "You're flirting with an ethics violation."

They both knew he'd gone way beyond flirting. He tried for a lighter tone. "I thought I was flirting with you."

"Your technique needs work." She checked her watch. "Where are they? I'm supposed to meet with the hotel wedding coordinator."

"Do you mind me asking what the hurry is?"

"I mind you asking on principle. But the truth is that I wanted to get married here and they had a last-minute cancellation. I could have the booking if I agreed to use all the bride's choices. There're too many dripping pearls and way too much netting, but other than tweaking the menu and canceling the karaoke machine, I can live with lilac and white."

So. Alexis was using someone else's wedding to marry Vincent. Could she be more unsentimental? Yes, Dylan did wish more of his clients thought with their heads instead of their hearts, but Alexis had carried it to the ultimate extreme.

"But can you live with this?" He picked up the contract and flipped through it. Folding it open to a section he'd hoped her lawyer would have flagged, he set the document in front of her.

She didn't even glance down. "We're not supposed to be negotiating the contract without my lawyer present."

"We're not negotiating. But due to the time constraints, I thought if there was language to which you objected, you could point it out and while I'm sitting here, I could get a start on making it more acceptable. It would save time." He tried one of his soothing smiles, which of course, she didn't buy.

"I would not dream of taking away any element of surprise that Margaret has planned."

"You're not supposed to be the one who's surprised." Dylan had begun to have doubts about Margaret. The clause in question could be interpreted as allowing Vincent to have mistresses in certain circumstances, the cost of which would be deducted from the payments due Alexis. Why hadn't she or her lawyer caught that? Had her lawyer been raised in a convent? Clearly, the woman had no clue as to the devious workings of the male mind.

"What do you care?" Alexis asked him.

He...just did. He didn't expect her to understand because he didn't quite understand. "Because I don't want to have to waste my time defending this thing in court when you realize what you've signed."

And that pretty much violated a whole slew of the canon of ethics. He'd get a few moral points, though, not that they would do him any good if Alexis reported him. He didn't think she would, but the fact that she could was bad enough.

As for Vincent finding out...Dylan would never practice law again.

"What do you mean?" she asked him.

He'd already said too much. "Look at it this way—you know what *you're* getting out of the deal, but ask yourself—what's *Vincent* getting?"

She gave him a slow, wide smile. "Me."

WELL, SNAP HER GARTERS if that wasn't the most impressive thing she'd ever heard in her life. And her death. A hundred thousand dollars a year. Sure, a dollar didn't go as far now as it did during Sunshine's life, but from everything Rosebud reported from reading newspapers, a hundred thousand dollars was a lot during this life, too.

The dark-haired woman with the awful haircut had not only convinced the silver-haired fellow to marry her, he was paying for the privilege. Well done. Sunshine applauded her, though Alexis couldn't hear her. It was always heartening to see a sister in sin make good. Women had certainly come a long way.

Sunshine sat on the back of the chair behind Dylan—nice Welsh name—and massaged his neck and shoulders. He wouldn't feel anything more than a vague relaxed feeling, but Sunshine thought he deserved some relaxing, poor tense baby. The man had itchy pants for Alexis, sure enough, and Sunshine was just in the right spot to know.

But Alexis was way beyond him. Alexis was looking out for Alexis and Sunshine was all for that. From what she'd overheard, it appeared that Mr. Cutie Pie here had had his chance and failed to take advantage of it.

His loss. Besides, for all his squawking, had he made a counteroffer? Not that Sunshine had heard.

Well, Sunshine's assignment was to make sure the bride and groom had no problems in the bedroom. Technically, it was to make sure they were happy and it was generally found that happiness in the bedroom meant happiness all around. However, bedroom or not, Sunshine was thinking *she* could be happy with a hundred thousand dollars a year.

DYLAN SAT ALONE in the conference and studied the magnificent view of the Rockies, which he appreciated not at all. What was the matter with him? Alexis had gone to her meeting and now Dylan waited for Vincent and Margaret to return. They all seemed very casual about this whole prenuptial agreement, which left him feeling unsettled. Squeamish. He rubbed at a tight spot just to the side of his neck and miraculously, it eased. Honestly, for all intents and purposes, this was a business merger and if the bride had been anyone else, Dylan would have applauded the match.

But the bride was Alexis.

ALEXIS LAY PRONE ON THE BED of a very quaintly decorated Victorian-style room, the charms of which were currently lost on her.

Alexis's eyes were closed and she'd taken aspirin to get rid of a throbbing tension headache caused by attempting to appear competent, in control and extremely hot while having her ex negotiate her future. She'd like to see anyone try that and *not* get a headache.

So? Did Vincent know she'd once dated Dylan or not? She couldn't tell.

She was long over Dylan. Yes, he was still attractive. No, she was not going to admit that the instant she'd walked into the conference room she'd remembered how his mouth had felt on hers. She wasn't proud of that. This guy had dumped her. Didn't she have more self-respect than to picture him naked the first time she saw him in seven years?

Dylan hadn't been the first to break her heart and he hadn't been the last, but was there any woman alive who wouldn't want to make a man who'd once dumped her kick himself when he saw her again?

Instead, she felt kicked. Just listening to him read the generous monetary settlement, with each year of marriage assigned a value in a way she tried not to find humiliating, was a strain. And she didn't want to justify why she'd agreed to the work terms. She understood why they were there—Vincent planned to have children after all this time and wanted to guarantee that his wife was around to raise them. And he was acknowledging the career sacrifice she'd be making by providing her with financial independence. He'd never wonder whether she was there because she wanted to be, or because she felt stuck.

Why couldn't everyone understand this?

And it wasn't as if she was completely abandoning her career in law. She was just off the payroll. Alexis had assisted Vincent for a long time and she expected she'd continue outside the office.

She wasn't going to think about it anymore. She was going to think about her wedding. Her lilac-and-white wedding. Lilac. The more she said it, the more it grew on her. Thank heaven it wasn't pink. She was not a pink person, but lilac, possibly with royal-purple accents—she could work with lilac.

And her family was coming in. She and Vincent, though mostly Vincent, were paying their expenses. She would see her parents, her grandparents, aunts, uncles, cousins and—mental drumroll—her sister and brother-in-law, along with three-year-old Madison, whom Alexis *would* get to see before her fourth birthday.

How wonderful that they were all able to stay a few days. How wonderful that they'd rearranged their schedules for her when she'd been putting them off for years and years…

Had she dozed off? Alexis sat up and quickly squinted at her watch at the same time she became aware of a presence in the room. A presence who was a blonde with old-fashioned sausage curls, red lips, a beauty mark and a great costume. Clearly, one of the hotel maids, probably trying to sneak in a fresh-towel delivery.

"Hi," the girl said. "I'm Sunshine. I didn't mean to disturb you."

"No problem. I shouldn't be sleeping now anyway."

"Oh, good. I've been wanting to meet you. I'm—" here Sunshine clasped both hands over her swelling bodice "—such a fan."

A fan? "I think you're confusing me with someone else."

"Oh, no. You're Alexis O'Hara and you're getting married Sunday afternoon, right?"

"Yes."

"I just admire you for the way you've taken charge of your life. Women make stupid mistakes because they don't think and they don't play to their strengths."

Well, yes, but what was she talking about?

"Don't depend on what a man tells you to get you in the sack. Make 'em pay up front. And you are."

Alexis gave her an icy look. "Are you referring to my prenuptial contract?"

Smiling widely, Sunshine nodded, her curls bouncing over her bare shoulders.

Alexis's jaw dropped. "Were you listening at the door?"

"Certainly not!"

Well, somebody had heard something and Alexis wasn't going to lower herself by questioning the hotel help. She would, however, inform the others. Vincent had a bad habit of talking loudly on his cell phone no matter where he was.

"Could I ask you a question?"

Alexis nodded.

Beaming, Sunshine bounced on the edge of the bed.

Alexis was taken aback. The maids were very friendly here.

Sunshine leaned forward, revealing an alarming expanse of pushed-up bosom. "How did you do it?"

"Do what?"

"Get him to keep paying!" Sunshine giggled. "Just getting him to marry you is what we all hope happens one day before we lose our looks, but how did you get him to agree to keep paying you afterward? Everybody knows it's supposed to be free then."

Alexis opened and shut her mouth. Twice. She should be offended, but this young girl was so good-natured and so eager and, well, the fan thing was flattering.

"I'm making a lot of money now and won't be working after I'm married."

"Exclusivity, yeah, I can see that. But marriage is usually enough."

"*That* is where women go wrong." Alexis warmed to her theme. "It should be enough. But what happens when you get a little older, you have a couple of kids and things begin to sag and hubby turns you in for a younger model? There you are with your best earning years behind you, and what have you got?"

The awestruck look on Sunshine's face was exactly the balm Alexis's frayed nerves needed. Her headache receded. Her self-confidence blossomed.

"And it's good for him, too," Alexis continued. "Think about it. He knows darn good and well you can afford to walk out of the marriage if you don't like it, yet you choose to stay. Frankly, it's got to be a huge ego boost."

Were those tears in Sunshine's eyes? "You're such an inspiration," she whispered.

Somebody finally got it. The last of Alexis's headache eased.

"You've got to meet Miss Arlotta."

Miss Ar—oh! That must be the wedding coordinator. Alexis was late. "I know." But how did Sunshine know?

"She's in the attic. I'll take you there."

The attic? There had been talk of choosing between two trellises. Maybe that's where they were stored. Alexis stood and stepped into her shoes. "Thanks."

"This is such an honor," Sunshine said.

She was piling it on pretty thick, Alexis thought, then wondered if maybe meeting Miss Arlotta was the honor. She might be very exclusive. Quite honestly, sometime last week, Alexis had stopped asking the price of things.

As they walked down the hallway, Alexis looked to the smiling girl bouncing along next to her. "Great costume."

"I know." Sunshine raised a diaphanous panel of the long wrapper she wore. "I was going for innocent naughtiness. The old guys love it."

The maid sure was blunt. "Good tips, huh?"

She shrugged a milky-white shoulder. "I did okay. Better than some, not as good as others." She poked

Alexis with her elbow. "They love it when they see something they think they're not supposed to be seeing. You might remember that."

"Uh, okay. I think it's a very clever marketing strategy for the hotel to play on its infamous past. I was looking at all the memorabilia in the little parlor downstairs."

"It was the high rollers' parlor. For the best customers and, of course, the best girls. Now, me, I figured it was the old guys and the widowers who had the money to spend and I got them to askin' for me special. Smart, huh?"

Listen to her. She was so into her part. Alexis was charmed. "Very."

"'Cause once I got to the high rollers' parlor, other high rollers could see me and some of them would ask for me, too." She looked momentarily wistful. "Some of them were mighty fine o' face. Like your beau."

Alexis knew she was referring to Dylan. Were there cameras in that private dining room? "How did you know?"

Sunshine stepped aside and indicated a door near the fire exit. "Attic stairs."

Alexis didn't open the door. "Sunshine, how did you know about Dylan?" If their privacy had been invaded, she wanted to know about it.

"I saw your face."

Her face? She'd always thought she was good about masking her emotions. And, hey, there weren't any emotions to mask here, at least not the nostalgic kind. "Was it obvious?"

"Only to me, honey."

A stranger could figure out that there had once been something between Dylan and Alexis? That was not good.

"Let's go," Sunshine urged.

Maybe she should bring it up with Vincent. That would probably be best, Alexis thought as she opened the door and started up the stairs. A casual mention that they'd dated in law school—but then he'd wonder why she hadn't brought it up before. As she'd explained to her mother, the problem here was that there was no problem and as soon as you tried to explain that there wasn't a problem, people immediately thought that there was a problem, only you were trying to hide the size of it.

Alexis was so lost in thought that she'd climbed halfway up an extremely dark and dusty staircase before the rickety handrail had her thinking that this couldn't be meant for guests. Talk about a lawsuit waiting to happen. She turned around to mention it to Sunshine. It was so dark, Sunshine nearly disappeared in the gloom. In a trick of what light there was, Alexis thought she could see the stairs right through her. She blinked.

"Just a little farther," Sunshine said.

"You should tell the manager to install more light here. I'm surprised the building inspectors have let this go."

"I don't think the building inspectors see this staircase."

"That's not really the point." Alexis came to the door at the top of the stairs. She reached for the old-fashioned door handle. "Is that original to the building?"

"As far as I know. I'll get the door."

Alexis never saw her touch it, yet the door creaked open. "That sounds like original hardware, too. I can't believe the owner isn't maintaining it."

And then Alexis forgot about hotel-maintenance problems because the sight of the attic room rendered her mute.

It was as though the picture of the former brothel's soiled doves, which hung in Sunshine's high rollers' parlor, had come to life. A group of young women, dressed in Victorian dishabille, lounged around boxes, trunks, old sheet-covered furniture and generations of castoffs.

"I—I thought this was a private meeting…"

"Hey, girls! Here she is! This is Alexis O'Hara."

A tiny dark-haired woman raised her arms in a swirl of vintage Chinese silk. "Brava!" She began to clap in the rhythmic European way. "Brava!"

The others began clapping, too. A redhead in cowboy boots and a bustier stuck two fingers in her mouth and whistled. "Yee haw!"

"You do us proud, cherie!"

"What's going on?" Alexis wondered aloud. Was this like celebrating a birthday at a restaurant and having all the waiters sing? Brides at the Inn at Maiden Falls get a send-off party from costumed maids?

"Yes, yes. She has done well for herself." A throaty voice boomed from behind a desk that Alexis swore hadn't been there moments before.

A woman with green-tinged skin, black eyebrows and yellow pin-curled hair sat behind the desk. She was only green-tinged because of the light from the green Tiffany-style torch lamp.

The girls quieted.

"I am Miss Arlotta," she announced. "You may approach."

Okay, so she was like a *really* exclusive wedding coordinator. Alexis decided to play along with whatever skit they were acting out and walked over to the desk. Up close, Miss Arlotta looked straight out of the Madams 'R' Us catalog.

Sunshine appeared at her side. "Miss Arlotta, Alexis has been offered a contract for marriage that pays her one—hundred—thousand—dollars a year."

More clapping erupted.

"In gold?" Miss Arlotta asked. She looked at Alexis. "Always make sure it's in gold."

Gold. Alexis just stopped herself from laughing. "That's good advice," she said, playing her role...of what, she didn't exactly know.

"And that's not all!" Sunshine clapped her hands together and gave a little jump. "She also gets the money she would have made if she'd been working."

Madam Arlotta sat back. "Well, now that is impressive."

"Maybe not so impressive." Alexis was being eyed by a sour-faced woman who plucked at the ties around her corseted waist. "Depends on how much she made."

"I'm very good at what I do," Alexis said.

The woman sniffed. "Hidden talents. Tricks. They always pay more for pervers—"

"Flo." The woman immediately went silent. "Alexis is our guest." Miss Arlotta stood and Alexis could see she was small for a woman with such a big voice. "We want you to know that though years and circumstances separate us, we celebrate what one of our own has accomplished for working women everywhere."

"I—thank you." This was just too weird.

"My Got. She vas showered viz more riches zan a royal courtesan."

"I thought you were a royal courtesan, Countess," Sunshine said.

"Zat is how I know zis." The woman shrugged the silk robe over her shoulders. "I consider you my equal."

Her equal? "And you were a courtesan?"

The Countess inclined her head. "Zat is so."

"Like...a mistress."

"Yes."

The skit wasn't as fun as it had been. "I'm not going to be a mistress. I'm getting married."

"And, honey, how you pulled that off without letting him sample the goods is what I want to know." This was from Miss Cowboy Boots.

"Glory, we always made them pay up front," Sunshine said.

"Wait a minute...wait just a little minute. This isn't amusing anymore."

They all looked blankly at Alexis. Not one broke character.

"You're—" she waved at them "—hookers. And you're implying that I'm a hooker, too."

"Honey," boomed Miss Arlotta. "You've established that you can be bought. You're just haggling over the price."

"I am *not* a—"

"Lady of pleasure?"

"Bawdy basket?"

"Nightbird?"

"Raspberry tart?"

"Flesh peddler?"

"Sportswoman?"

"Jade?"

"Harlot?"

"Pavement princess?"

"Pavement princess?" the others echoed and looked toward a girl wearing wire-rim glasses and a wrapper embroidered with rosebuds.

"I read and keep up with the times," she explained.

"Stop it everybody," Sunshine said, while Alexis still reeled from the barrage of insults. "You know she's way above us. She's like...a queen!"

"Did Dylan put you up to this?" Alexis could barely speak.

"Dylan's a former caller. He's carrying a torch for her," Sunshine told the group.

"He is not!" Alexis was momentarily distracted.

"He is, too. And he's downstairs right now, working his little heart out on your marriage papers."

"That's right. Marriage papers." Alexis drew herself up. "This is only an agreement so that there are no misunderstandings about what either of us expects."

"Hoo, boy! You expect a lot."

As they laughed, Alexis's head pounded again. "I'm going back downstairs. I have a wedding to plan."

"That's right. You don't want to lose him now, honey!"

More laughter followed her. She couldn't believe the hotel would allow a guest—especially one from whom they stood to make a great deal of money—to be so insulted. Maybe some brides wanted the full brothel theme for their wedding, but Alexis wasn't one of them.

And she'd find out who was behind this skit. She would. But right now, her head hurt and she was going to lie down, take more aspirin, and Miss Arlotta, or whatever her real name was, could just wait for her.

3

ALEXIS STOPPED BY HER ROOM to grab her coat and down that second extra-strength aspirin. Filling her glass from the bathroom faucet, she winced at the light, closing her eyes as she swallowed. Her headache was back in full force. Giving in for a moment, she sat on the bed. If this second aspirin didn't help, she was going to have to postpone the meeting. She couldn't make decisions right now. She could barely think.

Alexis dropped back onto the pillows and stared at the crown molding around the edge of the ceiling. She could feel her pulse pounding. Her eyes closed and then the phone, an old-fashioned, elaborately gilded rotary-dial affair rang, pounded, stabbed, her eardrums.

"Yes?"

"Ms. O'Hara, this is Tracy Wilman? From guest services? I have us down for a four o'clock consultation? It's four-thirty?"

"Is it?" People who only spoke in questions irritated her. Many things irritated her right now. "I'm not too happy with guest services."

"Oh? Shall I connect you—"

"No, sorry. Ignore what I said. I dozed off and I have a headache. Are you Miss Arlotta's assistant?"

"Who?"

Alexis blinked. "Never mind. Trellises, right? You mentioned that there were two?"

"Uh huh?"

"I'll be right there."

Alexis blindly cradled the phone. The handset clattered to the nightstand and she very carefully and very deliberately picked it up and placed it in the fancy golden holder.

What a dream. But so vivid and so real. And all Dylan's fault, of course.

The whole hooker thing just irritated her. Pre-nups were the smart thing to have these days, and Dylan with all his questions and innuendoes knew it. Why was he trying to make her think she was doing something wrong? He made his living writing pre-nups, for goodness' sake!

Alexis got her coat and took the stairs down in hopes that the exercise would clear her brain. Walking across the lobby, she paused at the historical parlor. Ignoring the furniture and framed clothing, she headed toward the large sepia-toned picture over the red-velvet chaise.

They were all there, just as they'd been in the attic. Well, not just as they'd been. In this picture, the women were dressed in fancy white or pastel street clothes and it appeared to have been taken outside next to the falls. Still, Alexis recognized Miss Arlotta— and there was a smiling Sunshine. Wow. She didn't remember studying the picture long enough to dream about the women in such detail.

Shaking her head—not a good idea—she made her way past the ballroom to the gardens outside.

"Tracy?"

A young blonde was directing two workmen to set up a trellis. "Ms. O'Hara?" She smiled in a way that reminded Alexis of Sunshine. In a way that made Alexis feel old.

"Call me Alexis. I apologize for keeping you waiting."

"No prob, you know? I went ahead and picked this trellis? You mentioned that you wanted understated and elegant and the other one is more elaborate?"

But Alexis had noticed a gazebo off to the side. "What about the gazebo? It looks like the perfect spot."

"The other bride chose a trellis," Tracy said firmly, making her first statement.

"Is there a rule against using the gazebo?"

"Flowers were ordered for a trellis?"

"Oh. Couldn't they just be...moved?"

Tracy flipped open her cell phone. "Yeah, it's Tracy at the Inn? Can you do the gazebo Sunday? I know. I know. I *know.*" She covered the mouthpiece. "The florist already started making the garlands for the trellis? The netting won't stretch?"

"I wanted to talk to you about the netting—I'm not that fond of netting, so let's take this opportunity to cut it out. We're going for elegant simplicity."

"What?" Tracy said into the phone. "The netting? There aren't enough flowers?"

"Whatever she's got—"

Tracy held up her hand. "You've got a lot of greenery you can use?"

"Greenery sounds great."

"She can try to get more flowers, but no promises?" Tracy looked at Alexis accusingly. "You did agree to no changes?"

"I didn't think this was that much of a change? But as long as we're talking about changes, how about adding a deep purple accent to pep up the lilac?" *Stop it. Stop it.* "Maybe go a little easier on some of the sparkly silver ribbon. I mean, as long as we're making a few adjustments."

"Did you hear that?" Tracy said into the phone. She narrowed her eyes at Alexis. "It'll be an extra charge?"

Oh, was that all. "I'm fine with that."

"Go for it." Tracy closed her phone.

"The gazebo seems more intimate," Alexis explained, but Tracy was jogging off to talk to the workmen. Alexis watched Tracy gesture her way, then she and the men glared at her.

For a hotel with a fabulous reputation, the customer service was sorely lacking.

"How's it going?" Sunshine called to her from a side doorway leading to the gardens. She gestured with a cup of hot tea. "You'll have to come get it. We're not allowed outside."

"Oh, thank you!" Alexis stared at her as she approached. "You're real?"

Sunshine eyed her warily. "Define real."

"Very funny. I fell asleep, right?"

Sunshine bounced her curls in affirmation.

"I had the strangest dream." Alexis sipped her tea.

It was sugared and she didn't usually go for sugar, but it was just what she wanted right then.

"You've cut out a lot of wedding fanciness," Sunshine said. "You know they're going to charge you anyway."

"I don't care. My wedding is smaller and needs to be scaled down."

"Don't scale down too much. You want the groom to know he's getting married!" Sunshine giggled.

Tracy was waving to get her attention. "They'll have to rewire the sound system?" she called. "Overtime?"

"I understand."

Tracy gave the men a thumbs-up before rejoining Alexis.

"I don't understand why most brides don't use the gazebo." Alexis turned to include Sunshine, but the girl had vanished back into the hotel. It was so sweet of her to bring the tea, though.

"The gazebo weddings are a higher-priced package?"

"Because of the extra flowers?" Alexis guessed.

Tracy nodded. "And extension cords, you know? They have to be hidden and secured, 'cause people might trip over them?"

"I'll try not to make any more changes."

Nodding, Tracy consulted her PDA. "Okay, so where's the groom? Vincent Cathy?"

"Cathardy."

"Oh? Where is he?"

"He's leaving all the arrangements to me." As she explained, Sunshine's words about not scaling down too much came back to her. Okay, fine. But the kara-oke machine for the reception was still out. She'd splurge on really fine wine, instead. The hotel had a renowned wine cellar.

"We're supposed to be running through the cere-mony?"

"Are we?"

"I think it's a good idea? The minister is going to be here at five o'clock?"

Just make a statement already, Alexis refrained from screaming. She called Vincent from her cell phone, but his line was busy. "I'll go see where he is," she told Tracy.

Alexis headed for the conference room by way of the lobby where afternoon tea was set up. She was putting her empty cup on a tray when the petits fours caught her eye. She took one of the delicate mouthful-size cakes, admiring the tiny pastel sugar flowers be-fore popping the whole thing in her mouth.

Her tongue crushed the sweet icing shell and rasp-berry exploded in her mouth. She sighed.

Sugar was making her feel a whole lot better than the aspirin. These were good. She hoped the wedding cake tasted as good. Maybe just one more. Look, there were chocolate ones. She hadn't noticed the chocolate cakes before. Were they as good? Only one way to find out. Her teeth sank into the cake. Ooh! They were tiny choc-olate-covered cheesecakes. Yum. Was that...amaretto? She'd need to taste another one to make sure.

Just then Dylan caught her stuffing petits fours in her mouth like a five-year-old.

He grinned. "I didn't remember you having a sweet tooth."

Alexis swallowed stickily. "Well, there's a lot you don't remember." Now she was thirsty. She took one of the china cups and filled it from a silver urn, leaving a chocolate thumbprint on the handle.

Casually, she wiped it off with one of the paper napkins and gulped down her tea. Burned her tongue, too.

"You eat when under stress?" Dylan asked.

"I eat when under hunger," Alexis told him crossly.

"Are you hungry now?"

"Not so much."

"Good. Then the petits fours will be safe when I tell you that Vincent is still hung up with that conference call."

"We're supposed to rehearse the ceremony." She checked her watch, noted a stray icing smear and was forced to retrieve another paper napkin. "I was on my way to get him."

"I see."

With as much aplomb as she could muster, Alexis tossed the crumpled napkin in the slops bowl where it bounced out, rolled off the edge of the tablecloth and came to rest by her feet.

Hoping Dylan hadn't noticed, she kicked at it and it stuck to her shoe. Of course it would.

Silently, Dylan knelt to pick up the napkin.

Sunshine appeared behind him and checked out the view. "Nice," she said.

Alexis's mouth dropped open—which didn't stop

her from looking—but Dylan acted as though he hadn't heard Sunshine.

"Why doesn't *he* rehearse with you?"

Had Sunshine made it her mission to eavesdrop on Alexis's business? "He can't rehearse with me!"

"What?" Dylan straightened and placed the napkin on the tray with the dirty cups and plates.

"You can't rehearse with me."

"You mean stand in for Vinnie?"

"*Vincent.*"

"Whatever." He shoved a hand into his pocket and leaned against the door frame. "I don't recall offering."

"I didn't ask!"

"You brought it up."

"No! She..." Alexis gestured behind him where Sunshine had been standing ogling him moments before. "Anyway, you can't."

"Why not?"

"I'm sure you're very busy." Alexis chose her most quelling voice.

Dylan refused to be quelled. "I'm not doing anything just now." He gave her a bland smile.

Bland smiles were the worst. They hid all manner of sneaky moves. "Vincent really should be the one to rehearse his own wedding."

"Now, *he's* busy. You should chat with him about prioritization. In the meantime, you've got me."

"I don't want you."

The words hung in the air.

Dylan regarded her somberly. "Yeah, I figured that.

Come on. One of you should know what you're doing."

This was a bad idea. Alexis didn't know why yet; she nevertheless knew it was. "It's not going to do any good for you to rehearse Vincent's part."

"Part," Dylan scoffed as he took her arm and began leading her back to the garden. "The groom just stands there. You at least get to make an entrance."

"Dylan..."

"Don't be embarrassed. You need a favor. I'm happy to oblige." He held her gaze. "Maybe someday I'll need a favor."

In debt to Dylan over something so trivial? Great. Alexis didn't like that at all.

"Hey, is this the groom?" Tracy gave him a professional smile when they met her outside.

"Alas, no." Dylan clasped both hands over his heart. "I'm only standing in. Hard as it is to believe, I'm still available."

"Oh?" Tracy's smile and body language warmed considerably.

Alexis's did not. "Let's rehearse. So where's the minister?"

"Right here." A woman about Alexis's age waved from the porch. "Just admiring God's handiwork." She gestured to the Rockies and came down the steps toward them. "I'm Joanna Martin."

Alexis couldn't ever remember meeting a minister who wore stilettos before. But then, how many female ministers had she met? She introduced herself, then felt compelled to explain Dylan. "This is my..."

"Friend is okay," Dylan inserted. "Fiancé's lawyer sounds clunky."

Alexis didn't look at him. "He's standing in for the groom."

"Do we need to wait a few minutes?" the minister asked. "We can."

"No. Vincent is on the telephone and will be a while. It's an important client," she felt compelled to add.

"It must be." The Reverend Joanna Martin was good at bland smiles, too. "We do need to discuss the ceremony before we start."

"The other bride didn't have a religious preference?" Tracy asked.

"My church is nondenominational, but I can certainly flavor your ceremony any way you wish," the minister said. "Up to a point," she added with a smile. "Do you have a religious affiliation?"

"I'm a Methodist. Lapsed," Alexis added for fairness.

"And Vincent?"

Alexis blinked. She didn't know. Had absolutely no idea. "He's...lapsed."

"I can do lapsed." Reverend Martin led the way to the gazebo.

"I've heard that's a very popular religion," Dylan said.

"Be quiet."

And he was, but Alexis could still hear him thinking. She was losing the bubble, that dreamy, fuzzy mental state that had allowed her to plan a wedding and envision her new life without letting certain details get in the way. Details like not knowing Vincent's religious preferences. Details she knew were there, but didn't want to deal with right away. She knew a lot about Vincent, make no mistake. They'd spent long hours together. She'd seen him angry. She'd seen him when he wasn't his best—and she'd been angry and not at her best around him, too. But she'd seen him looking powerful and attractive and charming and presumably, he felt she had a certain amount of attractiveness and charm, as well.

The thing was, all she had to do was gush about how much she loved him and giggle about how quickly it was happening and everyone would leave her alone and sigh and say how romantic it all was. But because she wasn't lying, people were constantly trying to burst her bubble.

Especially Dylan. Look at him. Silent as a reluctant witness, all he had to do was look at her the way he was looking at her now—with his eyebrow raised ever so slightly—and she could feel her bubble burst.

WELL, HELL. YES, HELL. Hell was standing here next to Alexis in a wedding that wasn't a wedding when he wasn't a groom. Or rather *the* groom. Her groom. Alexis's groom.

He'd been having groom thoughts. Not for long, but they were really strong groom thoughts. Dylan didn't even know there was such a thing as groom thoughts. No guy had ever mentioned them in his hearing—not even the grooms he'd known.

He'd been thinking about Alexis ever since he'd seen her name on the pre-nup papers. Then he'd seen her in person and those thoughts weren't groomlike in any way. Well, maybe in a honeymoon way. Definitely in a very specific, physical way.

He hadn't expected to feel such lust for her. Out-of-control lust wasn't really his thing. Controlled lust was great. To be desired even. He liked controlled lust. But this—this intense physical desire for Alexis was interfering with his work and his concentration. Making him act unwisely.

And then, and then he'd seen her eating those little cakes and he'd thought of wedding cake and feeding her wedding cake and, *boom*, groom thoughts.

Not good.

He hadn't spoken to her in seven years but the way he was feeling, it might have been yesterday. No. The day before yesterday. The day before they'd had the big breakup. Before all the hurt feelings and the ugly accusations.

Dylan felt as though his life had rewound to that point and instead of telling her it was time to go their separate ways, he *had* asked her to marry him. And this was the way he would have felt.

Not fair. Especially now that she was marrying someone else.

Who, incidentally, didn't deserve her. Not that Dylan deserved her, either, but he, at least, once had feelings for her. Apparently still did have feelings for her. Inconvenient feelings.

"The groom will stand here?" Tracy pulled him into place.

Tracy was cute and interested, and as the side of her body brushed his he felt nothing at all.

No, his feelings were reserved for the girl with the big eyes who was walking down the stone path toward him.

"We don't have the sound system set up yet, so could you, like, hum?"

Dylan started humming. Loudly. Anything to distract him from the vision of Alexis as bride. He added a little percussion by slapping his hand against his thigh.

"Dylan?" They were all looking at him, but it was the lady reverend who had spoken. "Maybe 'Trumpet Voluntary' and not Led Zeppelin?"

Hey. A lady reverend who recognized "Immigrant Song."

"I don't know 'Trumpet Voluntary.'"

"Then how about a rousing chorus of good ole 'Here Comes the Bride'?"

As if *that* would deflect any groom thoughts. But, he and Tracy and the reverend hummed and Alexis proceeded, holding an imaginary bouquet of flowers.

She looked luminous.

And right then, Dylan knew why all the newly married men of his acquaintance wore sappy smiles that turned into identical faintly amused ones whenever they were kidded about their lack of sexual freedom. They knew the secret. It was like being able to order off the menu at a great restaurant. Unlimited possibilities.

And Alexis was definitely off the menu.

"Will you have an attendant?" asked Reverend Martin.

"My sister," Alexis answered.

"Is she here?"

"She and the rest of my family won't be arriving until tomorrow."

"And the groom's attendant?"

"Yo," Dylan said.

Alexis stared at him. *"Yo? What is yo?"*

"Yo means I'm the attendant. Vinnie's best man."

"You can't be his best man! You don't even know him."

"He asked me." Apparently none of Vincent's male relatives could break away on such short notice. Dylan decided it was in the bride's best interests that he keep that to himself. "Besides, I'll waive my hourly fee. Call it a wedding present."

Alexis stood there with her mouth open—and still managed to look attractive.

"Maybe we should—" the reverend began.

"No. Let's get on with it." Alexis took his arm and resolutely turned face forward.

"Very well."

Dylan gave the reverend points for flexibility.

"At this point, I will say something about marriage in general and the family and friends who have traveled to witness..."

Alexis wouldn't look at him and Dylan couldn't stop looking at her. But he waited, knowing that at some point in the ceremony they would be facing one another.

"...and you'll hand your flowers to your sister and face Dylan—"

"Vincent. I'll be facing Vincent."

He could hear her teeth grind.

"Of course."

Alexis finally met his eyes and he knew he shouldn't be looking at her the way he was. She blinked, and at that moment the late-afternoon sun just cleared the branches of the trees to filter through the gazebo and send beams of golden light over them.

Dylan stopped breathing. Everything he'd given up to pursue his career was standing before him bathed in a lush golden light. He took her hand, wishing he could take back the years. Just touching her hand made his heart beat harder.

He absolutely, positively, could not allow this woman to marry Vincent Cathardy.

"OH, NICE WORK." Rosebud joined Sunshine at the doorway looking out at the gazebo.

"I just had to move the cloud the tiniest bit to get the sunlight in that spot. And isn't that a gorgeous color?"

"It reminds me—"

"I know."

They were silent for a moment.

"She's never looked better, if I do say so myself. And the way he's just staring at her..." Sunshine sighed.

"One little problem," Rosebud said.

"What?"

"They're not your bride and groom."

"I know!" Sunshine frowned, a rare occurrence. "I can't get the real groom out there! He is ignoring her to talk on that telephone contraption!"

"So cut him off. I taught you how."

"Yes, but I'm not as good as you are, and he just calls again."

"Do you want me to disconnect it for you?" Rosebud offered.

Sunshine hesitated. Having Rosebud help her might not mean a black mark in the Bedpost Book, but it sure wouldn't earn her any gold stars. And she was so close. So close. "No. I'm going to keep my eye on these two for a little longer."

DYALN LOOKED SO GOOD. And so not as old as Vincent. How shallow was that?

"And then you'll repeat the vows. 'I, Dylan—'"

"*Vincent,*" Alexis corrected through clenched teeth. And did he have to grip her hands so tightly? And rubbing her wrist with his thumb was completely out of line. She was going to ignore it.

"I, Dylan," he said, ever contrary. "Take you, Alexis, to be my wife."

She felt a pang in her heart—probably from one of the broken pieces. Well, her heart could just get over it. Her heart had had plenty of opportunities and look what had happened. Nothing. It was her brain's turn and look how well her brain had done—a distinguished, wealthy man who was ready to take care of all her needs and a whole lot of wants besides.

Dylan was one of her heart's former choices.

And what was the matter with him? Why was he looking at her that way? At first, she'd thought he was mocking her but now, she wasn't so sure. There was something about the catch in his voice just before he'd said the word *wife* that she didn't think he could fake.

But maybe he could.

As if it mattered. He'd had his chance and if he wasn't faking it, then he had a lot of nerve.

"I, Alexis, take you, Dylan—*Vincent*. Vincent, Vincent, Vincent. I take *Vincent* to be my husband. To have and to hold, for richer—" Was that a snort from Dylan? It was! He was mocking her.

Alexis yanked her hands away from Dylan's. "I think I can wing it from here," she told the minister.

"I'm sure you can." She closed the service book. "I'll read a scripture passage, if you have no objections."

Alexis shook her head.

"Then there will be the exchange of rings and the usual statement that you're married and that's it."

"What about the 'you-may-now-kiss-the-bride' part?" Dylan asked.

Alexis glared at him.

"Of course." Reverend Martin smiled. "And don't forget to get your flowers from the maid of honor afterward. Think 'kiss and turn.'"

"That's not what I'd be thinking," Dylan said.

"We all know what you'd be thinking," Alexis snapped.

"I might surprise you." And he drew her toward him and lowered his head.

Alexis was caught off guard. That was it. Really, a woman is rehearsing her wedding, and a man pretending to be the groom kisses her on cue, and, well, it's understandable that in her confusion, she kisses him back.

That was her story and she was sticking to it.

But before she came up with her story, there was the kiss. Dylan bending toward her was familiar. She forgot the fact that it hadn't been familiar for some time. She tilted her chin automatically, and by the time she remembered where she was and what she was about to do and with whom she was about to do it, it would have been more awkward to stop than to turn this into a little thank-you kiss. Except her lips...kind of stuck. On his. And it became the little thank-you kiss that could.

It was chilly outside in spite of the waning sun and Dylan's lips were cold at first—a little shock in addition to the great big shock of discovering that Dylan was kissing her not in a hey-I've-still-got-it way, but in a last-chance-to-change-your-mind way. In other words, he was putting a lot of emotion into this kiss. If she didn't know any better, she'd think he was trying to send her a message.

This was a very pleasant way to communicate. He'd refined his technique a little, but so had she. The kiss went straight to her head. Well, and other parts, but primarily to her head with dizzying speed. Her hands, her cold hands, encircled his neck and she melted into him.

There shouldn't have been any melting with Dylan and she'd already begun unmelting when there was a significant clearing of a pious throat.

With a mighty push, Alexis unglued her lips from Dylan's. "Very funny, Dylan." She took a wobbly step backward.

"It wasn't meant to be funny."

No one is laughing. "You're going to give Tracy and

Reverend Martin the wrong idea." She turned to the two wide-eyed women. "We're old friends."

"Indeed," said Reverend Martin. She stepped forward and handed Alexis her card. "In case you have any...questions." She held Alexis's gaze. "Or would like to talk."

"Thank you." Alexis managed a credible smile, which she held until the woman climbed the steps to the porch.

"Aren't you the wicked one?" Tracy playfully swatted Dylan's arm. She leaned toward him and lowered her voice, but not so much that Alexis couldn't hear. "I've got a meeting with a couple planning a birthday party but I get off at seven?"

"That's nice," Dylan said.

"It can be." And off she went, without acknowledging Alexis in any way.

Alexis lit into him. "How could you do that?" A best defense and all that.

Dylan smiled slightly as he looked down at Alexis. "I gave her no encouragement whatsoever."

"I'm not talking about her, I'm talking about you kissing me!"

"I wasn't the only one kissing."

"But you started it."

He gave her a look he had no business giving her. "Yes, I did."

The cold seeped through her jacket. Alexis rubbed her arms and started for the side door. "Was that supposed to be some kind of fidelity test? Did Vincent put you up to it?"

"You've got issues with Vincent that have nothing to do with me. The kiss was all my idea."

"It was a rotten idea!"

"I'm thinking it was a good idea," he said. "Maybe one of the all-time great ideas. I learned a lot."

So had Alexis. She'd learned that she'd missed him and hadn't even known it.

They reached the door, which Dylan opened for her. Alexis stomped in, then turned to face him. Address the main issue head-on and dispose of it before it has a chance to gain strength. It was a strategy she'd used before and she was going to use it now. "You proved that I'm attracted to you. So what? You already knew that. It changes nothing."

He took a step toward her, his gaze searching hers. "It could."

Alexis willed her face to go blank. "Not if I can help it." On that note, she brushed past him and headed for the stairs and her room.

Just before she was out of earshot, she heard him murmur, "What if you can't?"

4

ALTITUDE SICKNESS, that's what it was. The signs were all there—dizziness, butterflies in the stomach, shortness of breath—nothing more than altitude sickness and not a visceral reaction to Dylan's kiss.

He'd just had lack of oxygen on his side.

Instead of going to her room, Alexis changed her mind and tracked down Vincent. She needed a dose of oxygen-heavy Vincent. She found him in the hotel's business office commandeering a printer.

He glanced up—maybe half a second. "Everything on track?"

Alexis felt the first stirrings of irritation. She'd been very understanding when he hadn't made the rehearsal or met with the minister, not that he'd known about that, she reminded herself. But if he'd been there, then Dylan wouldn't have been playing groom. "I met the minister. She—"

"She?" That got his attention.

Her irritation grew. "Do you have a problem with that?"

"Never thought about it." He shrugged and went back to plucking paper out of the printer tray and reading it nearly as fast as it was printed.

Alexis had been going to ask Vincent what religion he practiced or didn't practice as the case might be, but having seen him in work mode before, she knew this wasn't a good time for a theological discussion.

"Everything is fine." *If you don't count me kissing my former lover, who just happens to be your lawyer, and liking it quite a lot.* "We're meeting the chef tonight, though the menu is pretty much set."

"Hmm."

"So I'll see you at dinner, then?"

"Uh..." Vincent stared at his watch. "I might have time for a quick—damn!"

A clunking crunch announced a paper jam. Judging by the evidence in the trash, this wasn't the first time. Vincent yanked open the printer top.

"I can barely get a cell connection," he complained. "The faxes are unreadable. The computer is antiquated and all the files I need had to be converted to an ancient form of MS Word and this hotel has a dial-up Internet connection so downloads are taking forever."

"It's a sign." Alexis tried a little prewifely rub on Vincent's arm. She'd never touched him in any way but a few social cheek pecks. "You're just fated to take the weekend off for your wedding."

"Come on, Alexis." He stopped just short of shrugging off her hands. She pulled them away immediately. "Don't go all sentimental on me now."

Right. No sentiment. She backed out of the room. "See you at dinner."

ALEXIS SAT IN THE GOLDEN RULE, the hotel dining room, which was decorated in a kind of brothel-lite style. Some red velvet, a little gilt and dark wood. She wished Vincent was there to see it. They could snicker and feel superior together.

"I like for the bride and groom to sample their wedding supper." The chef stood over her after personally delivering pâté in the shape of a wedding bell. But that was nothing. The butter was sculpted in the shape of doves. "At the wedding, they remember very little. They usually eat even less."

Alexis smiled and refrained from telling the chef that it wasn't that sort of wedding and she, personally, would be ravenous.

"Also, I understand that you wish to select wines to go with the meal? I might be able to make some slight adjustments to the menu, since the meal isn't for so many people. The Inn has an excellent cellar."

Alexis gave him a genuine smile. Vincent was a bit of a foodie and he did love his wines. They'd have a good time exploring the wine cellar tomorrow.

The chef clasped his hands together and looked around. "I had hoped to meet the groom, but I must return to the kitchen. Please send word when you're ready to begin. In the meantime, you have your champagne."

Alexis held it up, though she'd sipped none of it.

He gestured. "And some salmon mousse to start. Such a lovely color for weddings."

Pink. Salmon pink, but pink just the same.

The chef seemed to be waiting for her to taste it, so Alexis did so even though she hated to spoil the bell shape. "It's yummy." At the chef's stiff smile, she realized she should have said something more sophisticated, but she'd been more concerned about starting to eat and not being able to stop. The altitude was making her so hungry.

Only the bow that had been on top of the bell and one slice of crusty bread was left when Dylan loomed over her thirty minutes later. She'd actually drunk one glass of champagne, then refilled the glass herself so it would look as though she'd waited for Vincent.

Now, she looked up at Dylan. "Are you the messenger of doom once more?"

"No." He sat down, though she hadn't invited him. "I was about to eat dinner. I'd asked Margaret to dine with me, actually, but she, too, has the phone glued to her ear. She's not staying at the hotel, you know."

"There wasn't room," Alexis said tightly. She didn't want him sitting here, eyeing the champagne. Eyeing her.

"She said it was a good thing since Vincent is hogging the computer and printer."

"This hotel doesn't have business facilities as such."

His fingers crept toward the champagne flute. "I suppose they figure most people have other priorities on their honeymoon."

"I was the one who wanted to get married here." Alexis responded to his implication that Vincent was shirking his groomly duties. "We only had a week's notice. I had to choose between getting married this weekend and waiting months."

"Or getting married somewhere else. Say, Houston? Where you and your friends and business associates live?" He frowned. "Not too many of them could make it, could they?"

The groom could barely make it. Alexis stared at the

pink salmon bow on the plate. "My friend Marisa was married here. She said it was magical. She said..." Alexis swallowed, surprised to find herself choking up. Horrified that she was doing so in front of Dylan. "She said afterward she was more in love with her husband than she ever dreamed she could be. They try to get away at least once a year and come back here. But it's hard to get bookings. So, when I was told about the cancellation..." Why did she tell him all that? She'd just revealed herself to have a weakness for sentimentality.

"Hey." Dylan picked up the flute. "Here's to weddings and honeymoons." He gave her a buck-up-old-girl smile.

Rather than scold him for drinking Vincent's champagne, Alexis picked up her own glass and clinked against his.

"Hmm." Dylan grimaced. "Warm and flat. Hope that's not a sign of things to come. Or not, as the case may be."

"Just when I think you have a modicum of class..." Alexis signaled the hovering waiter. She meant for him to bring a fresh glass for Dylan, but the man scampered off to the kitchen no doubt to mistakenly alert the chef. Alexis groaned.

Dylan misunderstood. "No problem. I'll just have some of yours." Before she thought to protest, Dylan picked up her glass and drained it. "Nice stuff."

"Dylan!"

"Hey. If Vincent shows up, I'll buy you another bottle."

"*When* Vincent shows up, I'll let you."

There was a look on Dylan's face that meant bad news for Alexis.

"Just tell me," she said.

"I was waiting for a fax." Dylan looked into the bottom of the champagne flute. "I saw him in the office. He was eating a sandwich."

"Vincent doesn't eat sandwiches."

"Okay, it was an open-faced focaccia with provolone and grilled portabello. They're great. I had one for lunch."

"I didn't have lunch," Alexis mumbled.

"In that case, drink up." He refilled her glass. "Maybe I can get you drunk and have my wicked way with you."

Alexis picked up her champagne and eyed it. "You do have a wicked way about you."

As Alexis drank, the waiter brought the salad, as she'd suspected would happen.

"The ever-popular mesclun. Good for splattering and getting dark green bits stuck in your teeth." Dylan unfolded the napkin and put it in his lap.

Alexis didn't object to him joining her. What would be the point? "It's nutritious."

"This is a wedding supper. It's not supposed to be nutritious."

"The other bride chose the menu." Nice raspberry vinaigrette dressing on the salad. Alexis would have chosen the same thing.

"Doesn't it bother you to use someone else's wedding?"

"Not at all. It saved a lot of time and effort."

"Are you wearing her dress, too?"

Must maintain serenity. "No."

"Did you even buy a wedding dress?"

"Yes." To forestall any more questions, she added, "It's a lovely strapless crepe and tulle with a re-embroidered beaded and sequined Schiffli-lace sheath with a demitrain. Would you like me to describe the veil?"

"Let me be surprised." Dylan's eyes had begun to glaze over at the word *tulle*. He tilted his head to one side. "Am I annoying you yet?"

Alexis responded with a cool, serene little smile. "No."

"I'll have to try harder then."

Alexis's fork clattered to the plate. "Why do you wish to annoy me, Dylan?"

"To see if I can." He spoke with unnerving intensity. "To see if you're still capable of feeling anything."

"You know what I feel?" She leaned forward. "Relief. Relief that the whole dating thing is behind me. Relief that I don't have to try to meet anyone else, get to know him without wasting too much time ferreting out his shortcomings and then deciding if I can live with them or not. It's been 'or not' every time."

"Maybe you're too picky."

"Maybe I am. It doesn't matter anymore."

"Maybe it should."

"Why?"

He didn't answer, but his eyes softened.

She knew that look. She'd seen that look before and not just from Dylan. "Because of *you?* You think I'm dooming myself to a loveless marriage because I couldn't have *you*?"

Dylan spread his hands.

"Oh, please." What a colossal ego. Spying the waiter headed their way, Alexis straightened. "You did hear what I said about feeling relief just then? That was relief and not regret."

"I've been thinking," he began.

"That's always a bad idea."

"What if? Do you ever think about that?"

"Not for oh, say, six-and-a-half years."

He looked surprised. "It took you six months to get over me?"

"And I am over you." Alexis rolled her eyes and drank more champagne.

"I'm not sure I'm over you," he said softly. Seductively. Dangerously.

Alexis narrowed her eyes and growled.

Their server and an assistant arrived with two plates of food which they showed to Alexis and Dylan. "Your guests will be offered a choice of chicken breast with wild-rice pilaf and a vegetable medley or beef with mushroom sauce and roast potatoes, also accompanied by a vegetable medley."

"Will the veggies be singing a different tune with the beef?"

"Dylan."

"I'll take the chicken. She looks as though she's in the mood for red meat and gnawing on bones."

"Sir, our beef cuts are boneless."

"Pity."

"He's not the groom," Alexis told the server. "So you don't have to feel sorry for me."

"Trust me," Dylan said. "You'd feel sorry for her if you saw the groom."

"But we thought..." The server trailed off with an expression of acute distress. "Madam should have said something."

"It's fine." Alexis sawed at her meat. "The groom couldn't make it and I was hungry."

She stabbed the meat chunk with more force than she intended.

"See that?" Dylan gestured to her. "Never get caught between a hungry bride and her meat."

Alexis, chewing with great deliberation, glared at Dylan.

The server fled.

Dylan could barely suppress a smile. "So, Alexis, how long are you prepared to delay the wedding if Vincent is on the phone?"

Alexis stared at her plate as she finished chewing and swallowed. She'd like to say her appetite fled, but it didn't. Pesky altitude. "Dylan," she began very carefully, "what is it you hope to accomplish by making these snotty remarks? It's hard enough to overlook your professional lapses, but what I choose to do with my life isn't any of your business. We have had no direct contact since law school and if Vincent hadn't hired you, you wouldn't have given our marriage— assuming you even heard of it—any thought at all."

Dylan picked little bits of things out of his pilaf. "Well, he did hire me and I am thinking about it. I'm thinking you turned out to be just as brilliant as I thought you would be. You're even more beautiful now than you were, and you have the potential to be a powerhouse female attorney."

"Always the qualifier," she murmured.

"A powerhouse any kind of an attorney," he corrected. "If you plan to give that up, then you ought to do it because you're crazy in love and can't figure out any other way to be together. But you're not crazy in love. You're just crazy." He abandoned the pilaf and ate a bit of chicken.

"It's still not your concern. How's the chicken? I'm thinking a big red would really beef up—so to speak—this meal."

"You want the truth?" he said so seriously she was afraid to nod.

But she did.

"I expected the food to be better."

So had she, but that wasn't what they'd been talking about. "We don't always get what we expect."

"Remember that." After holding her gaze for a moment, Dylan abruptly turned into the ideal dinner companion.

Alexis would have enjoyed the meal if she hadn't been examining everything he said for double meanings and verbal traps.

They'd always been able to talk about anything and the years hadn't taken that away. Alexis laughed and was immediately aware that it had been a long, long time since she'd done so.

Did Vincent ever laugh? She couldn't remember. Laughter was important, wasn't it? Well...well...she and Vincent didn't have a laughter kind of relationship. Not yet. She thought of Vincent's reaction to her hands on his arms. She'd meant to offer comfort and support, the comfort and support a life partner would offer as a matter of course. It had felt awkward to her and clearly even more awkward to him.

Their relationship still felt the same as it always had, and Alexis instinctively knew it had to change. She expected a physical relationship with him—how else was she supposed to have children? But aside from that, she, well, she liked sex. Good sex. Something that, lately, had been in very short supply.

Dylan could always be counted on for good sex.

Ack. Wrong.

He smiled across the table at her just then and the candlelight caught his eyes in such a way that they glowed. He found her attractive and wasn't bothering to hide it. Was the man trying to commit career suicide? One word from her—but he knew she wouldn't say that word.

She placed her napkin beside her plate. "I think it's time for me to leave."

"You can't leave now." His voice was husky.

"You can't stop me."

"But Madam must taste the cake!"

While Alexis had been making eyes with Dylan, their server appeared. She hadn't even noticed. "I forgot about the cake."

The server tried unsuccessfully to hide his surprise. "There are several fillings that the chef has selected. You may have any combination or have the cake as it is here. He will bake it tomorrow, so before you leave, please let him know your preferences. We have lemon, Grand Marnier, hazelnut, raspberry and cappuccino." With a flourish, he set down a miniature wedding-cake top, complete with plastic bride and groom.

Alexis plucked them out immediately. "These must go, never to be seen again."

The waiter didn't blink. "Is there some symbol that would have meaning for you that we could create? Some people have a pet or a representation of the place where they met."

"How about a cell phone?" Dylan suggested.

Alexis ignored him. "Flowers, either real or icing, would be fine. A plain top would be fine. Anything else would be fine."

The waiter handed her a cake server wrapped in a large tulle bow with lilacs stuck in the knot. The ends trailed across the icing. Alexis jerked the thing off the knife and tossed it on top of the plastic bride and groom. "Silver has such a lovely clean look all on its own."

"Understood, madam."

Alexis wished he'd quit calling her "madam." It made her think of the attic dream and the woman with the blond pin curls. *She'd* never put up with tulle. Alexis cut into the cake.

"Hey, don't be stingy with the cake," Dylan said. "And you have to remember to give Vinnie a big enough hunk so it won't fall apart before he smashes it in your face."

"There will be no cake smashing." She handed him the plate.

"Where's the fun in that?" Before she knew what he planned, he broke off a piece and held it out to her.

"You don't expect me to fall for that." Alexis leaned back out of cake-smashing reach.

"I wouldn't do that to you." He still held out the cake.

"Right. You expect me to believe that when you just told me smashing cake into someone's face is fun?"

He leaned forward. "Trust me."

"Why—" She'd been going to say, "Why on earth should I trust you?" but found her mouth full of cake.

Glorious cake. Sugary cake. Raspberry and Grand Marnier melted together to become something greater than they were apart. Yes. That was the combination.

"Mmm." She closed her eyes as the sugar melted sweetly with the raspberries, adding enough tartness for interest, and the Grand Marnier cloaked the whole thing with a subtle richness. She swallowed and licked her lips. More. She must have more.

"You really do like your cake." Dylan's voice was strangled.

Alexis sighed. "It's wonderful. Have some."

"I'm not really much of a cake—"

Alexis broke off a piece and popped it into his mouth, returning the favor.

Only Dylan's lips closed around her fingers. When she pulled, he sucked on them, so she stopped because it felt good though she shouldn't be feeling good with Dylan. Not this kind of good.

But of course that still left two of her fingers in his mouth.

His hand clamped around her wrist and he let one finger escape. He drew his tongue along the other.

Alexis felt a tingle zinging down her arm straight to her belly. Tingles had also been in short supply lately.

Watching her face, Dylan gently sucked all the icing and cake off her finger. And Alexis let him.

Yeah, she did, even though she knew he was making trouble for reasons he'd not explained to her satisfaction. He was stirring things up. Things that had gotten a little sludgy from lack of use. This was like starting a car that had been sitting in the garage for a while and letting the oil run through the system to lubricate all the parts.

And the way Dylan was looking at her and doing interesting things with his tongue was sure enough making *something* run through her system. Her motor was purring. Not revving, but definitely purring. Just what she needed.

She'd consider this a test to see if she could separate desire from...from desire. No, that wasn't right. She was separating desire from *Dylan*. That was it. Desire was just fine. Dylan was not.

In fact she hoped he would get caught up in his little game. Then when she married Vincent, Dylan would feel some of the same hurt and rejection she'd felt.

The trick was not getting caught up in the game herself. The way Dylan looked at her made it difficult to remember that she was an engaged woman. When he let her pull her remaining finger from his mouth and pressed a gentle kiss on the palm of her hand, she figured they'd both had enough. Probably scandalized the server, too.

"I—I'm leaving. Now." Alexis stood, took two steps away, then turned back and picked up the rest of the cake.

She was going to need it.

AFTER SHE LEFT, Dylan forced himself to eat a few bites of cake. Alexis had asked him what he was doing and he honestly didn't know. Committing career suicide most likely if he kept poking around in old embers to see whether any sparks flew.

The sparks were flying on his part, that's for sure. He couldn't help himself. For some reason, he felt an unreasonable attraction to her—more than when he was dating her all those years ago. He supposed he was trying to see if she felt anything for him. He suspected she did.

Okay, so what? What now? What about tomorrow? What about the day after tomorrow? And what if Alexis ditched Vincent for him?

Sure that was a stretch, but was that what he wanted? Dylan sure didn't want her marrying Vincent, but what else did he want?

Until he knew the answer, he'd better cool it. Otherwise, he was nothing more than an old-fashioned cad.

ALEXIS SAT IN HER ROOM and scarfed half the cake. "Cake" implied that it was bigger than it was—at the most it was the size of two jumbo muffins. Okay, maybe three, but it wasn't a real, full-size cake. Anyway, it was either binge on cake or call her mother again.

And…and there was the matter of her motor still running. Shouldn't she go for a test-drive?

Dylan had forced Alexis to confront the physical aspect of her relationship with Vincent—namely that there wasn't one. Frankly, she hadn't thought it would be a problem. She and Vincent had both been working like mad people this week in order to steal away for the wedding. In her mind, she'd downplayed the importance of the honeymoon, assuming…assuming too much, probably.

Maybe she should visit Vincent tonight.

If she could find him.

5

VINCENT WAS IN HIS ROOM. Alexis could hear his voice through the door. She hesitated, then knocked.

"I don't need turn-down service," he called.

There was turn-down service and then there was *turn-down* service. "It's Alexis."

The silence went on longer than she would have liked. After a few murmured words, Vincent opened the door.

"Hi. I—"

He held up a finger and responded to the person on the telephone. "Hang on."

This was not the reaction she'd hoped for.

Hurrying back to the table next to the window—it clearly wasn't meant to be used as a desk—Vincent rooted through piles of papers.

He hadn't invited her in, but he had opened the door. That was good enough for Alexis. She entered and closed the door behind her.

His room was smaller than hers and there was only one chair. He'd dragged the burgundy wing chair over and was obviously using it.

"You still there?" He wasn't talking to Alexis, thank goodness. Stooping, he went through the piles he'd stacked beneath the table.

Alexis had a lovely lady's escritoire in her room and

she wasn't using it for anything more than a catchall. She considered offering to switch rooms with Vincent, but didn't, and she wasn't particularly interested in examining her motives just then, either.

She had other motives to worry about.

"Here it is." Vincent stood. Not easily, Alexis noticed.

She casually wandered farther into the room and skirted the bed. Feeling awkward and hating that she felt awkward, she forced herself to perch on the corner of the bed. She was his fiancée. They would shortly be sharing said bed.

"Yeah, give me a sec." Vincent sat in the chair and grabbed for a pencil. Alexis watched him try to hold the tiny cell phone next to his ear with his shoulder and write. Several times, he rolled his shoulders.

Alexis moved from the corner of the bed to the arm of the chair. "Here. Let me," she whispered and began rubbing Vincent's shoulders.

Vincent exercised and kept himself in shape, but Alexis's first impression was a bony scrawniness. But she forgot all that at the look of irritated surprise Vincent threw at her.

"Just a minute, Jerry." He muted the phone. His expression reminded her of the one he saved for first-year interns he thought had been stupid. "What are you doing?"

Alexis slowly dropped her hands and let a few beats of silence go by during which she maintained her own expression—one that reminded him she was *not* a first-year intern.

Fortunately for their future, he caved first. "Sorry,

Alexis." Vincent rubbed his forehead. "This whole Briarwood thing got very tense all at once. Be patient just a little longer."

"Just a *little* longer." She smiled and gave his shoulders one more quick rub before standing. As she did so, she noticed a heated glimmer in his eyes before he returned his attention to the phone call.

All right. She'd been looking for that glimmer. That particular glimmer was very reassuring. She should encourage that glimmer.

And she knew just the way to do it. "See you in a minute."

Back in her room at her closet, Alexis removed the negligee that she'd been saving for her wedding night. It was neither bridal white nor vixen black, but a very naughty dusky peach ivory. The satin slip gown was elegant, glamorous, and it made her look completely naked at first glance. At several glances even. She'd pretend not to be aware of the fact, which should get Vincent's motor running.

She changed into it and studied herself in the full-length mirror. She was looking good. Although she hated to spoil the surprise, she really thought she ought to seduce Vincent tonight.

She'd brought some candles with her for atmosphere and ripped off the plastic wrapping before stowing them in an overnight bag she'd bring to the room with her.

Vincent's room was on the floor above her near the end of the hall by the stairs. Surprise was the plan. She wanted to appear at his door in her naked negligee. Vincent, the phone probably still glued to his ear, would be rendered mute. He would stare. She would smile and sashay past him into the room, a cloud of expensive...

Alexis dug in her luggage until she found her cologne and squirted herself. Now, where was she? Right. Trailing heavenly scent past Vincent.

He'd stare. He'd babble something into the phone and flip it closed.

"Alexis!" he'd breathe in pleased surprise.

She'd give him a coquettish look over her shoulder. Coquettish. She should practice that. She looked over her shoulder and tried a little smile. No, not that one. She tried again. Hmm. Coquettish and the naked negligee didn't seem to go together. Better go for sultry or blatantly come-hither sexy.

She found sultry much easier. Okay. Sultry it was. She would give him a sultry look as she placed the candles on either side of the bed. She'd light them and purse her lips as she blew out the match. Matches. She needed matches.

Unless she had matches in her suitcase left over from a previous trip, Alexis didn't have any matches with her. Just in case, she checked the drawers in the room.

No matches. Though he didn't smoke, Vincent carried a gold lighter given to him after some big-deal case. So, she'd give him the sultry look, turn back around, hold out the candles and in her huskiest voice ask, "Got a light?"

It always sounded good in the movies. Then, if Vincent wasn't already attempting to ravish her, she'd position the candles on the nightstand and sit on the bed.

Surely he would have gotten the idea by then.

Enough rehearsal. After that, she'd improvise.

Alexis stuck her head out her door and looked up and down the hallway. Deserted. Excellent.

The only tricky spot was passing over the balcony that linked the original brothel to a newer addition. She'd briefly be visible to the entire lobby and if anyone looked up, they'd see her in all her faux-naked glory.

Cautiously, Alexis ventured out into the hallway.

So far, so good. Confidently, she set forth, prepared to brazen it out with anyone she encountered. She made it to the open balcony and peered around a pillar.

A couple with their backs to her was looking at the display in the historical parlor. Good. Someone was noodling on the old-timey upright piano. Bad, since he faced her.

Worse, it was Dylan.

She'd forgotten that he played; he'd never had much time for practice while they were in school.

He'd worked hard, she remembered, and not just for himself. How many study groups had he been in? She'd wanted to see him, so she'd tagged along, even though she'd already mastered the lesson and knew he had, too. Everyone wanted to study with Dylan because he had a knack for distilling the conflicts in court cases to their simplest elements.

She could hear him now, reminding them to figure out what was truly important to each side. Not necessarily what litigants said they wanted, but what they really wanted. Sometimes they didn't even know themselves.

Alexis supposed he still had the knack.

She stepped out from behind the pillar so she could see him better. He was always more empathetic than she. She'd been guilty of thinking it was a sign of wimpiness.

She closed her eyes as she remembered lecturing him on how he needed to toughen up. Not too long after that, he'd broken up with her. It was such an uncharacteristically ruthless move that Alexis hadn't thought he'd had it in him.

The thing was, once she'd stopped indulging in self-pity, she'd admired him. It's what she should have done.

Dylan was playing little bits and pieces of things, sounding out forgotten passages by ear. Apparently tiring of that, he stood and opened the piano bench. After rifling through the sheet music stored inside it, he found something he must have liked and reseated himself at the keyboard.

Alexis had lost her best chance. She should have snuck across the balcony while he was searching through the piano bench.

But she'd been looking at him. Remembering. Also remembering the feel of his shoulders as she'd rubbed them after a long study session.

So different from Vincent's.

And remembering where those shoulder rubs had led.

Also different from where rubbing Vincent's shoulders had led. But Alexis was going to give Vincent a second chance.

In a minute. Or two.

Dylan started playing a Scott Joplin rag, slowly picking out the notes and without the usual bouncy rhythm, but Alexis could still recognize the tune, though she didn't remember the name.

She wondered what he'd been doing the past seven years. Sure she'd heard of him professionally, but she wondered how he'd fared personally. Had he dated a lot or just a few women for a long time? Was he in a relationship now? She couldn't imagine him in a relationship with anyone else. Simply couldn't. Or was that simply wouldn't?

At that moment, Dylan looked up and caught her eyes. She felt a thrill go through her. Honest to Pete, what did it say about her that Dylan could arouse her more with a look than Vincent ever had?

The music stopped. Dylan's chest rose and fell. So did his eyes. His gaze roamed over her and still, he didn't move. He didn't even blink. If she didn't know better, she'd swear he'd gone into a trance. Well, yeah! This was the reaction she was going for. Good to know...

Alexis stopped in the middle of a breath having just remembered that she was standing there in the naked negligee.

She took one very large step backward so that the pillar hid her once more and listened for the music to resume. When it didn't, she swore under her breath and ran for her room.

Dylan didn't know her room number, did he? But if

anyone could charm it out of the receptionist, Dylan could.

And so Alexis was back in the clothes she'd recently changed out of and had stuffed her negligee into her purse when the knock came at the door.

She fluffed her hair, licked her lips and opened the door.

Dylan stood there, breathing as though he'd run up the stairs, which he probably had. "I just hallucinated you naked. You know anything about that?"

"No."

"So you weren't naked?"

"No." Alexis stepped into the hall and pulled her door shut behind her.

"But you were on the balcony just now."

"Yes. I'm on my way to see Vincent." She gestured down at herself. "Fully clothed."

"The balcony is in that direction." He gestured ahead of them. "Your room is here."

"I forgot something." Alexis grabbed her purse and started walking.

Dylan followed. "Like your clothes?"

This was very near the truth, but Alexis was not going to explain. "I'm not an exhibitionist and I'm not responsible for your hallucinations." As she walked past the balcony, she didn't look down.

"Too bad," Dylan said as she opened the door to the stairwell. "You look good naked."

Alexis smiled to herself as she began climbing the stairs. "And so, as I recall, do you." She visualized him staring after her, mouth agape. At least he didn't follow her.

The encounter with Dylan had gone much better than she would have thought. It put Alexis in a confident mood when she knocked on Vincent's door. Yes, everything was in fine working order. Now, if it would just work for Vincent. "It's Alexis," she said, before he could ask.

She heard creaking and then the door opened. "Yes?" he asked as though she were some member of the hotel staff. Not the hooker maids, but say, a bellman.

He was dressed in paisley pajamas. Probably silk and very traditional. The gentleman in his retiring clothes. Fussy. Alexis could see that she'd have to loosen him up. Well, that could be fun, couldn't it?

He didn't invite her in. Drat. She wished she was wearing the naked negligee.

"May I come in?" She hated having to ask.

"I was in bed."

"Excellent." She brushed past him and kicked off her shoes.

Vincent still stood by the door. Alexis sat on the bed and patted the spread next to her. "You look all done in. Briarwood giving you trouble?" She purposely introduced the case because that gave them a common starting ground.

"Family-owned companies are more trouble than they're worth." Vincent sat next to her with a sigh. "Even worse is when two of the families are friends and are sharing a cabin on an end-of-season ski vacation."

"They aren't!"

"They are."

"Turn around and let me rub your neck muscles." Alexis kept her voice matter-of-fact.

She appreciated what he was doing—up to a point. Vincent was allowing her to take the lead so she wouldn't feel pressured into a physical relationship before she was ready.

Actually, she was ready now. Instincts told her they needed a prewedding night. Something to bond them together before tomorrow when they would face their gathering families. Or Alexis's gathering family. She still didn't know who of Vincent's clan would be able to come.

Just her family would be more than enough. Alexis knew she'd be better at convincing them she was happy to marry Vincent after a night in his arms.

He tilted his head back. He did have nice thick hair. "That feels good." Alexis kept massaging and Vincent started talking about the merger. All three families had to agree and it appeared that two families were ganging up on the third. The silly people were trying to keep it from Vincent, as if they could. Vincent was brilliant.

But perhaps too close to the case.

After hearing him talk for long enough that her hands, inexperienced at massaging, were starting to feel the strain, she said, "Why don't you call the third family and let slip the information that the others are holed up in a cabin in Wyoming drinking too many hot toddies? They might not know."

"I hadn't thought of that." He looked off into the middle distance.

"You represent all parties, so it couldn't be considered violating any confidentiality. That way, the third group can plan a trip to Wyoming, if they feel like it, and you can get married in Colorado in peace."

"That sounds delightful, but maybe too optimistic."

Alexis boldly turned her back to him. "I've had a long day, too. My shoulder is bothering me right there." She indicated a spot at random and waited, anticipating the feel of Vincent's hands on her for the first time.

She felt the weight of them settle on her shoulders and then his thumbs pressed just above her shoulder blades. Alexis winced. Okay. Massage wasn't one of his strengths. He had others.

She thought aloud to distract herself. "Also, what do those other two families want? Why are they merging with a larger company? Money? Increased marketing? Why are they trying to cut out the third family? Do they think that third group is negotiating with someone else?"

"Good points."

Hmm. She was going to have to stop the business chat.

"I knew there was a reason I made you my assistant."

"And now I'll be your wife." She turned around, mainly so Vincent would stop bruising her shoulders, and smiled up at him.

"I'm very lucky," he said lightly and she knew he was going to kiss her.

It was a nice kiss. A bit proper for her, but probably best for a first time. He pulled away, but Alexis placed her hands on either side of his face and gazed purposefully into those sharp blue eyes of his.

Then she drew his lips to hers and kissed him. Really kissed him. Waited for a response. Waited to feel something.

Vincent raised an eyebrow. "Are you sure?"

When she nodded, this time he drew her to him and delivered a technically perfect kiss.

Alexis was so relieved; she hadn't been aware that she'd been holding her breath. As long as the technique was good, the rest would take care of itself. She gave him a brilliant smile. "I'd like to change."

"By all means." He lay back against the pillows and yes, indeedy, that gleam was there.

Still, Alexis wasn't quite up to changing in front of him. She escaped into the bathroom and leaned against the door. Thank heavens he seemed to know what he was doing.

This was going to work. Relief made her giddy. She slipped into her naked negligee and tousled her hair. She wished she'd thought to bring the candles, but had left them in her room. No matter.

She turned out the light and opened the door.

Vincent didn't move. She smiled. The sight of her had stunned him.

There was a gargling snort. Omigosh! She'd given him a heart attack!

Alexis raced to the bed, but Vincent was not having a heart attack. Neither was he stunned.

He was asleep.

She clasped her hand over her own racing heart. *She* nearly had the heart attack.

Well, hell. What now? Wake him? Crawl into bed with him? He was flat on his back and his jaw had eased open. This was not an attractive look for him.

"Vincent?" she called softly.

Nothing. Except another grating snort.

While Alexis regarded her future husband from the foot of the bed, deciding whether or not to wake him, the phone rang, taking care of the problem.

Vincent came awake instantly and reached for the phone, clearly having forgotten that Alexis was in the room. She moved into his line of sight. His expression didn't change as his gazed raked over her.

He covered the mouthpiece. "Honey, I'm going to be a while. I missed dinner. Would you check with the kitchen and see if they could bring some crackers and cheese or something?"

Crackers and cheese? He preferred crackers and cheese to Alexis in the naked negligee? She backed away. "Sure. I'll just..." She hooked a thumb toward the bathroom.

Well. This was a failure on multiple levels. First, Vincent had ignored the naked negligee, the same negligee that had caused a very gratifying reaction in Dylan.

Second, there was the whole "honey, can you get me a snack?" thing. He'd already eaten. If he'd wanted privacy, all he had to do was ask. And what was with taking a phone call when they were about to have sex for the first time?

And the way he'd covered the mouthpiece instead of pressing mute. By covering the mouthpiece, he knew that the other man could hear him. The "honey" was to let the man know that Vincent had a woman in his room. A woman he could order to get a snack. Grr.

So once again, she was back in the clothes she'd traveled in. She'd left her suit jacket in her room, but because she was in a skirt and because Swineheart, Cathardy, and Steele was a very conservative firm, Alexis was wearing conservative pumps and pantyhose.

As she sat on the edge of the tub and struggled back into them, she swore that once she was married, it was self-tanner and waxing.

Or pants.

DYLAN COULDN'T SLEEP. He also couldn't get the image of a naked Alexis out of his mind. He would have sworn in court that she'd been standing there wearing absolutely nothing. Why she should do that, he didn't know. When they'd dated, she sure hadn't been into the public-risk thing.

Clearly, his thoughts about her were getting harder to control. It didn't help that he found himself with time on his hands. He should have brought more work with him, but frankly, he'd thought this was going to be a one-day turnaround. He'd already changed his return flight because Vincent had asked him to be his best man.

And what the heck was that about? Just casually throwing it out there between phone calls. Expecting that Dylan had no other demands on his time.

And, because he was Vincent Cathardy, Dylan had cleared his schedule, thus reinforcing Vincent's sense of entitlement.

Wow. Best man to Vincent Cathardy after negotiating his pre-nup. Dylan's stock was going to rise. He'd immediately called the managing partner of his firm who had been speechless for a full fifteen seconds. Dylan had timed it. The man had pretended to be studying Dylan's client schedule, but Dylan knew he was just flat-out speechless.

He'd thrown in a little something about being an old school buddy of Vincent's fiancée, then wondered if he should have. It wasn't a secret, but he didn't want to make trouble for Alexis.

Okay, he did want to make trouble for Alexis, but not that kind of trouble. He just desperately wanted to shake her out of whatever trance she'd gone into.

She'd once, within his hearing, been described as ruthless and it had been a high compliment. Alexis would have made a great defense attorney because a defendant's guilt or innocence never figured into her strategies. But she'd gone for corporate law.

That was beside the point, Dylan thought, wandering around until he ended up in the kitchen. The point was that she was prepared to give it all up for Vincent Cathardy. As far as Dylan could tell, she wasn't being blackmailed or forced into anything. Nor was she in love with him.

It made no sense.

Neither did his sudden renewed attraction to her.

Dylan made his way over to the stainless-steel counter where a snack tray had been left for guests to help themselves. Cookies and milk. When was the last time he'd had cookies and milk?

He poured himself a glass from the thermal carafe,

grabbed a chocolate-chip and a macadamia-nut cookie and sat on one of the dining stools around the cook island.

His life had been chugging along just fine before this weekend. Why would a few hours in Alexis's company point out the hollowness of his existence?

He worked hard, but not excessively. He had friends he saw semiregularly, and he dated when he felt like it, which, to be honest, wasn't all that often.

He may, he admitted, have become jaded about marriage, having seen so many breakups, and that might have caused him not to pursue it.

Dylan munched on his cookies and figured that maybe it was time he sought a relationship. One for the long haul. He'd have to find someone on the traditional side, since he couldn't see them both maintaining high-powered careers once they had children. And, honestly, he didn't want to be the primary caregiving parent. He'd be happy to make enough money so his wife could take a few years off.

He did note with irony that it was the pattern Alexis was going for, but he didn't understand why she had to be paid for it. Marriage was a partnership. A settlement in case of a divorce was fine by him, but Vincent was paying her not to work.

And what if she never got—

Pregnant. Maybe he was wrong about her physical relationship with Vincent. Maybe she was already pregnant. His mouth was full of white-chocolate macadamia-nut cookie as he had this thought and it was hard to swallow. Both the cookie and the thought.

But why? Why was he so bothered? He *had* to get over this. He had to get over Alexis.

And that was the moment Alexis came striding into the kitchen, looking particularly Alexis-like in that confident way he remembered. She was a woman who could make things happen. He pitied the future PTAs and Booster Clubs she'd run because Alexis didn't have time for inefficiency.

She saw him, paused, then continued over to the snacks.

Dylan took a drink of milk. "Are you a hallucination?"

"Am I naked?"

"No."

"Guess not, then." She grabbed a sandwich roll and split it open.

Dylan smiled down at his cookie. "Got the munchies?"

"Even if I did, I wouldn't eat this late at night." She slapped some mayo on one piece of bread.

He watched her hesitate between the bright hot-dog yellow and the gourmet brown grainy mustard. She opted for the brown kind, slapping it on the other piece of bread.

"So Vincent has the munchies."

"So it would appear."

Trouble in paradise? "Why doesn't he just nibble on you?"

Alexis stiffened and Dylan knew she was glaring at him even though she faced away from him.

"I remember how you taste," he said softly. He

couldn't help himself. Truly. It was as though some-one else was speaking for him.

"Stop it, Dylan."

Excellent advice. So why was he slipping off the bar stool and padding over to her? "Alexis, are you pregnant?"

She whirled around and he caught a slice of cheese in his stomach. "Don't sneak up on me!"

He peeled the slice off his shirt and tossed the cheese in the trash. "Are you?"

"You do realize it's none of your business."

"Not necessarily. If you're pregnant, I would advise my client to request a paternity test and address the issue in the pre-nup."

Her eyes did the blank thing. "You are despicable."

"Not yet, but I can be." He grasped both her arms, hauled her to him and kissed her.

Even he hadn't expected the kiss.

The shock of touching her held him still, and Alexis, as well, he reckoned. He recovered first. In a moment, she'd push him away, and tell him off. Maybe even slap his face, which he deserved. He'd feel better if she slapped his face.

But this meant he had to work fast. Was the way he'd felt after the other kiss a fluke? Did they still have something that should be investigated?

Dylan angled his head and nudged her lips, surprised when they parted. A wave of feeling washed over him, much more intense than what he'd experienced during this afternoon's impulsive kiss. The kiss felt comfortable, right. The familiarity of her kiss was a turn-on for him. Who knew?

He held her closer and fully explored her mouth and then he felt her soften, felt her arms creep around his neck. Felt her kiss him back.

Past memories and present sensations merged. He couldn't tell what was an echo of the passion they'd once shared and what was a brand-new passion born this weekend.

One or both of them would regret this.

Oh, Alexis, he thought. *I was absolutely insane. We could have been together all this time.*

And they could be together now.

Except that she was getting married. To someone else. To Vincent Cathardy.

She sure wasn't acting like it, though. She was supposed to push him away and act the affronted maiden, not encourage him. Not cling to him as though she never wanted to part. Not simulate the horizontal mambo with her tongue in his mouth.

At that moment, Dylan knew he could have her back if he wanted. Instead of making him feel triumphant, he felt sick. What did he think he was doing? He had no right. No right to have her abandon her wedding because Dylan was having second thoughts about something that happened seven years ago. He didn't know if this was an echo of their former love or love again.

The timing, as usual, was all wrong.

He pushed her away abruptly.

She looked shell-shocked. "Dylan..." She held out her arms and he stepped out of reach.

They stared at each other, and for once Alexis's eyes were full of emotion. Desire for sure. Maybe something more. Something he wasn't going to put a name to and wasn't going to acknowledge.

But as long as it was there, Dylan knew he wouldn't be able to leave her alone. She would have to be the one to put a stop to this.

He made a derisive sound. "You were supposed to slap me, not stick your tongue down my throat."

Her face froze.

"Well? Go ahead. Slap my face." He forced himself to continue deliberately. "It's what Vincent's fiancée should do."

Betrayal, then understanding crossed her face. He waited and there it was—contempt. At her expression, Dylan felt something inside, something that could have been wonderful fade away.

"I don't want to touch you," she spat and ran from the room.

She well and truly hated him now. As she should. There would be no more kisses and no more what-ifs.

Problem solved.

6

OH, WAY TO GO, ALEXIS.

How could she have kissed Dylan? Again! How stupid. Kissing anyone other than Vincent was disgraceful under the circumstances, but Dylan was his attorney, which meant it was especially dim-witted.

Not good. Not good at all.

And the look on his face. He'd despised her for being weak enough to respond to him. But not as much as she despised herself.

She fled to Vincent's room and was halfway there before she remembered the sandwich she'd left in the kitchen. Well, he didn't eat the sandwiches anyway. Besides, she intended to make Vincent forget all about his snack while she forgot all about Dylan.

She knocked on the door and kept knocking—she really should get her own key—until he opened the door.

Pushing past him, she mouthed, "Hang up the phone."

Vincent shook his head and she drilled him with a look. "It's eleven o'clock at night. We need to talk."

Evidently he knew she meant business because he watched her warily as he concluded his conversation. Alexis could tell he wasn't happy about her tactics, but she figured he'd forgive her in a few minutes.

He flipped the phone closed and put it on the bed-side table. "Now, what's so urgent?"

"This." Alexis literally flung herself at him.

He was caught off guard and fell against the bed, his silk pajamas causing him to slide. She rolled off him and Vincent, with his hair mussed for the first time in Alexis's memory, looked at her in shock. "I thought you said we needed to talk." He smoothed his hair as he regained his seating on the bed.

"I lied." And she kissed him. Hard. Aggressively. She would erase Dylan's kiss from her memory. She *would*.

She pushed forward and he, gently this time, fell backward with Alexis splayed on top of him. Almost in self-defense, he rested his hands against her back.

As she'd established earlier, Vincent could kiss. Now if he'd only kiss with more enthusiasm. Alexis ran her hands up and down his chest, hoping he'd move his hands against her back. Elsewhere, too, but her back would be a good beginning.

"Alex—"

She kissed him quiet and attempted to unbutton the buttons on her blouse. A little skin on skin should help. Trying to lever herself off his chest so she could work her hands between them, she caught him in the ribs with her elbow.

He winced.

"Sorry." Why wasn't *he* unbuttoning her blouse? Maybe because she hadn't given him a chance. She bent over him hoping he'd finish the job.

He rubbed a place beneath his ribs. No. He should be rubbing *her*. She leaned down and kissed the spot where her elbow had poked him, then worked her way back up to his mouth.

"Al—"

And *why* did he want to talk? Alexis didn't want to talk. She wanted to get this over with. She untied the sash on his robe and it fell open. Vincent had chest hair. *Gray* chest hair.

She closed her eyes and ran her fingers through it. Okay, so Vincent had gray chest hair. Big deal. She'd think of it as silver blond. Platinum blond. That was it. She trailed kisses down his chin and neck.

"Alexis." He gripped her hips.

All right. She moaned to encourage him. Fake, of course, but she could fake interest. Unfortunately, Vincent could not.

And after several moments, situated on top of him as she was, Alexis was aware of a crucial missing element. She pretended not to notice.

"Oh, Vincent," she said in a nice, breathy, nearly-overcome-with-feeling kind of voice. "I need a few minutes to get ready." And perhaps he might get ready, too, she thought.

She slithered down the bed to the floor, stood, and began unbuttoning her blouse as she made her way to the bathroom, just so he'd know what he was getting ready for.

Then she shut the door, leaned against it and closed her eyes. This was beyond disaster. Was he...was he the "i" word? She couldn't even complete it in her mind.

"What am I going to do?" she murmured aloud.

"Well, I can give you some tips, if you like."

Alexis yelped as her eyes flew open. There, sitting on the edge of the whirlpool bathtub, was Sunshine. She was examining Alexis's negligee, which hung on the hook behind the door.

"I didn't know you were in here!" How embarrassing was this? "Why didn't you say something?"

"Looked like you were doing fine."

"I mean to let us—me—know you were in here!"

Sunshine laughed. "I didn't want to interrupt."

"But we...we..." Alexis's toes were curling in embarrassment.

"Oh, honey—" she waved away Alexis's stuttering "—it ain't nothing I haven't seen before."

Alexis squeaked. That must have been what Vincent had been trying to tell her, though not very hard she remembered, then drew her breath in sharply. What if he was one of those men who wanted to be watched? Oh ick, oh ick, oh ick.

"And I gotta tell you, you've got a bigger problem than modesty."

"Right now, I can't think of what it might be." Alexis was blushing and she didn't need to look in the mirror to confirm it.

"Your hubby-to-be has a case of the limp willies."

This was not happening. She wasn't here. She didn't know where she was, but she certainly wasn't in Colorado in Vincent's hotel bathroom talking to the maid about...about...

"But you're in luck."

"Oh, do please tell me how."

"Older men are my speciality." Sunshine dropped the hem of the naked negligee. "They love me. And

I'm real good at encouraging them, if you know what I mean."

This was surreal. "I really don't think we should be discussing this."

"Honey, you need to be discussing it with somebody."

True. Oh, so very true.

Sunshine leaned forward. "We're just a coupla girls talkin' shop here."

Alexis cleared her throat. "About that—"

"You were on the right path earlier just talking to him," Sunshine went on. "Sometimes the thought of it kinda scares them, you know?"

"You were here then? But...but where..." Alexis had a very horrible, ugly thought. "Does this room have cameras in it?" She yanked open the door. "I'm going out there to search the bedroom and if I find a camera, this hotel is toast."

And then Sunshine was in front of her blocking her way. But that was impossible. Sunshine was behind her. Then again, impossible was only an opinion because Sunshine was indeed shepherding Alexis back into the bathroom.

"How did you do that?"

"Isn't that cool? I had to practice really hard. People think if you're a ghost you can just do all that disappearing and reappearing and moving stuff around automatically. But you can't! You have to learn that just like anything else. But then again, you have a whole lot of time to learn it." Sunshine sighed. "It's been over a hundred years. And I'm still not the best with the new stuff. I mean, everytime I manage to figure out how something works, something else is invented. Telephones without wires? Who knew? And don't get me started on computers. We don't see many of those here, except the ones for reservations and the one in the office, but Rosebud—you met her—dark hair with the glasses? Well, she likes to read and keep up with all this. Me, I like to stick with the tried and true. I'm pretty good with weather. I can make sure it's not raining or anything for your wedding." She smiled.

Oh, goody. The maid was a babbling lunatic and Alexis was alone in the bathroom with her.

If she screamed, would Vincent rescue her?

She mentally tried out that little scenario. Vincent, lying in bed trying to, er, anyway, he hears a scream, struggles out of bed, takes the time to retie his robe, shuffle into his house slippers and call, "Alexis?"

And in the meantime, Alexis would be strangled by a delusional blond hooker with sausage curls. She probably had a ribbon, or a tie or something hidden in her hands even now.

Okay. Alexis was on her own. "It sounds like you've had an interesting time of it," she said soothingly as she edged to the side, hoping Sunshine would move and she could dart to the door.

"Oh, you don't know the half of it."

Alexis didn't know any of it, but had a feeling she was going to find out.

"I'll tell you the story sometime, but right now, you've got to get out there and prove to that man why you're worth all that money."

Alexis opened and closed her mouth. Best not to argue. She nodded mutely. "I'll go now." She walked to the door and had her hand on the knob when Sunshine's voice stopped her.

"You don't believe me, do you?"

"I—"

"How can you not believe me when I introduced you to everybody? We've never done that before."

Sunshine looked so hurt that Alexis couldn't just walk out on her. "I believe that *you* believe you're a ghost."

"Darn tootin'. You see, Miss Arlotta—you met her—wanted this fancy, schmancy chandelier to class up the place. It was a gas chandelier and took nine months to get here all the way from gay Paree. Well, them boys that were supposed to hook up the thing got kinda distracted, you know?"

Alexis nodded. "Men haven't changed much." What was she saying? She shouldn't encourage her.

"They did something wrong and the gas leaked out. It was a Sunday, and we were always closed on Sundays. It was a good day. Our picnic day." A wistful expression crossed her face. "Anyways we went to sleep that night and when we woke up, we were dead."

When they woke up, they were dead. Of course. "I read about the 1895 gas leak downstairs." Sounded as if Sunshine had, as well.

"It took us a while to figure what was going on, I'll tell you. We're trapped here. We can go up on the roof where we used to sit out so the men could see us, but we can't leave the building. When this place was shut down, we took to hanging around the attic. First this was a boarding school, then a store, and then, about ten years ago, it was converted into a hotel. There's the old part, the original house, where your room is and this new part they built. Anyway, that's when Judge Hangen—he happened to be visiting Miss Arlotta that night—told us that we could redeem ourselves by helping couples with the physical expression of their love.''

"How do you know when you're redeemed?" The question just popped out.

"Miss Arlotta and the Judge and a council decide. We each have to help ten couples. Miss Arlotta keeps track in the Bedpost Book. If we're really good, we get a gold star. If we break one of the rules, we get a black mark. Too many black marks will erase all the good we've done.''

"I see.''

"And, I—" Sunshine placed both hands over her ample chest "—have been assigned to you and Vincent. I know I've already said this, but it is an honor.''

Assigned? Alexis didn't know about the ghost bit, but she did remember the fabulous romantic reputation of the Inn at Maiden Falls. The place was booked months in advance. "And all of you help others, too?''

"Yes." Sunshine bounced her curls.

"Well...nobody ever says anything about ghosts.''

Sunshine gave an unconcerned shrug. "People will believe what they want to. Besides, what are they going to do about it? Just 'cause they don't think we're ghosts doesn't mean we aren't.''

Something was wrong because Sunshine was beginning to make sense. "You don't look like a ghost.''

"Oh. You mean like this?''

As Alexis watched, Sunshine began to appear

foggy. Alexis blinked, but Sunshine's image didn't clear.

"Boo," she said.

"Boo? You're kidding."

"I thought it would help."

Alexis almost laughed. "I'm sorry, I just don't..."

And then Alexis swore she could see the bathtub behind—through—Sunshine. She closed her eyes. "Don't." Sunshine must be using some kind of hallucinogenic gas. A little squirt and, presto, instant ghost.

Alexis hoped there weren't aftereffects.

"You're not mad, are you?"

Alexis opened her eyes to find a very concerned—and solid—Sunshine. "Of course I'm not mad."

"Oh, whew. I can't afford any more black marks. Not when I'm so close."

"Then you'd better quit sneaking up on me. And no hanging around when I don't know you're there."

Sunshine gave her a disgusted look. "I don't, like, spy on you when you're changing your clothes or nothing. What do you think I am?"

"Is that a trick question?"

Peals of laughter erupted from her. She looked so young and so happy and so full of life. She made Alexis smile. Yeah, older men would be attracted to her because she would make *them* feel young and happy.

"Okay." Alexis took a deep breath. She couldn't believe she was going to do this. "So what do I do about Vincent? I mean, I want children. I never thought I wanted children all that much, and I know you think I'm getting lots of money, but I was making lots of money." Alexis knew how Sunshine thought she was making that money, but just let it go. "So there's no point in changing my life if Vincent can't, well, you know."

"Well, that's easy enough to figure out. Take a seat." Sunshine closed the lid on the toilet and gestured for Alexis to sit on the tub. That meant Alexis was farther from the door, but at this point, she didn't care. She sat on the edge of the tub.

"What you do is cuddle up to him until he falls asleep. Then you take a bit of ribbon and tie a slipknot around his sugar stick. And in the morning, if the knot has slipped, then you know the flesh is willing, but the spirit is weak."

Vincent with a ribbon around his..."What if he wakes up?"

Sunshine giggled. "Tell him he's won first prize and take it from there."

Alexis gave an unwilling laugh, and then another one, not so unwilling. She clamped a hand over her mouth. The image of the powerful Vincent Cathardy with a ribbon—didn't the florist mention lilac ribbon? No. Alexis simply must not think of it ever again.

She gave one last giggling hiccup, then cleared her throat. "But seriously. If you have any hints in that direction, I'd love to hear them."

What followed was a frank and enlightening discussion. Alexis soaked it all up, too desperate to dwell on the fact that she was getting sexual tips from the maid.

She stood. "Okay. I can do this."

"Of course you can!" Sunshine floated over to the naked negligee.

No, she didn't float. She was merely light on her feet.

"This is absolutely perfect." She took it off the hanger and held it against herself. "The color makes me blush!"

"I thought it was pretty sexy."

"So put it on." At Alexis's look, Sunshine rolled her eyes. "I'm going, I'm going."

"Really going? And no eavesdropping?"

"How will I know if you need help?"

"Because I will tell you all about it *afterward*." Had she really just promised that?

"All right. No need to get your knickers in a twist." Sunshine walked toward the door.

"Wait! He'll see you."

She smiled. "Not if I don't want to be seen."

"Let me look." Alexis quietly cracked the door, and then pulled it open a little more.

Vincent had turned off all the lights except one of the bedside lights leaving the edges of the room in shadow. Oh, good. He must be reading, and once he had his glasses on, he didn't see much past the printed page.

Alexis opened the door wider, then gestured behind her for Sunshine to sneak past.

When nothing happened, Alexis looked over her shoulder, but Sunshine was gone.

Wow. She *was* good. Alexis had been concentrating on Vincent so much, she'd missed Sunshine leaving.

Alexis hurried to put on the negligee. She'd been in

the bathroom for so long, she considered just walking out naked, but remembering Sunshine's advice about keeping things gradual and subtle, Alexis pulled the thing on for what she hoped would be the last time. Honestly, she was going to wear it out at this rate.

Turning off the light in the bathroom, Alexis quietly opened the door.

Well, this was it. Show time.

She approached the bed. Vincent had, indeed, been reading. Part of Alexis was miffed, but she reminded herself that an indefinite amount of time had passed while she'd talked with Sunshine.

She hoped Vincent hadn't overheard them because she sure didn't have an explanation if he had.

And then Alexis watched Vincent's head slowly nod forward.

Not again. "Vincent?"

No response. Alexis stood by the bed and gently tugged the papers from his loose grasp.

Some things just weren't meant to be.

Alexis slid the big, old-fashioned black glasses from his face, turned out the light, gathered her clothes and snuck back to her room.

DON'T LEAVE! What was the matter with that girl? Did she listen to nothing Sunshine told her? What about the cuddling? How about the ribbon? At least she could have tied on the ribbon, even if she didn't want to stay.

Sunshine started to appear in front of Alexis in the hallway, but didn't.

Sunshine recognized that look of relief on Alexis's

face. She'd felt it, herself, on more than one occasion. And so she let Alexis go back to her room while she thought about what that look of relief meant.

WAS IT POSSIBLE TO GET a cookie-and-milk hangover?

Dylan rubbed his stomach and looked at the depleted pile of cookies. His first official binge.

"Mmm. The cookies are popular tonight."

He hadn't heard anyone come in. A blonde, wearing a getup that made her look like an eighties backup singer for Madonna, peered at the cookie tray, then at Dylan.

He wondered if he looked guilty. "Have one. They're real good."

Smiling, she walked over to him. "You're a friend of Alexis's, aren't you?"

After what just happened, was he still? "Yes. Are you?"

"I'd like to think so."

"Are you here for the wedding?"

"I work here. I saw you rehearsing with her."

"I'm the best man."

The woman gave him a long look. "Honey, I'm beginning to just wonder if you aren't."

ALEXIS WOKE UP EARLY the next morning, determined to try again with Vincent. He was tired last night. But this morning, all systems should be go.

However, when Alexis got to his room, Vincent was packing.

Had she scared him away? Or did he think less of her because she wanted to sleep with him before the wedding?

He *was* older and more conservative...but wait a minute. He'd grown up in the era of free love.

"What's all this?" she asked.

"Alexis, it's impossible."

Her stomach clenched. "No! Vincent, we can make this work. I'm sorry if I came across as too aggressive last night."

"No, no, no, no." He stopped packing and gave her a quick kiss. On the forehead. "You were delightful. I...was distracted."

Comatose, more like.

"Then why are you leaving?"

"Because I cannot get a decent connection—landline or cell phone. The Internet seems to be down all the time and the faxes cut off midway through. It's impossible," he said again. "I'll just take a puddle jumper to Wyoming and save us all time."

"You're going to *Wyoming?*"

"It's not far. We're already in Colorado. I'll be back by noon tomorrow."

"Tomorrow! Three hours before the wedding?"

"That's plenty of slack time." He grinned. "You won't start without me, will you?"

"But...but we have friends and family coming in today. What am I supposed to tell them?"

"I know that you are capable of greeting them without me at your side."

"But it would be very nice to have you at my side." She abruptly switched tactics. "And there is the prenup to finish negotiating."

"You and Dylan work it out," Vincent said as his phone chirped. "Alexis, could you arrange for a breakfast tray to be sent up and finish packing for me?"

He turned away and Alexis understood that it was a rhetorical question.

Well. Pack? For him? She didn't know him well enough to pack for him. Then she laughed inwardly at the irony of it.

It sounded very wifely. Very servile. She wasn't sure she wanted to set that kind of precedent.

She gave herself a mental slap. Here he was, frantically trying to get away so that he could get back and she was quibbling about throwing a few things in a suitcase.

Alexis used the room phone to call for breakfast, ordering a large one, which Vincent could eat or not as he chose. Then she just added everything in the closet and drawers except his wedding clothes to the suitcase and zipped it shut.

Vincent was gone before his breakfast arrived, so Alexis ate it. Every bit, including bacon which she hadn't eaten in years.

Clearly, she must never, ever live in high altitudes.

After gorging herself on pork products, she called Margaret and went in search of Dylan to finish with the pre-nup.

She was not looking forward to facing Dylan again.

She'd deliberately avoided thinking about him and the way he'd kissed her.

What a jerk. That was so unlike him, too. Even when she'd been terribly hurt, she'd never thought of him as a jerk.

She left a message on his voice mail to meet her in

the lobby where she was going to arrange for use of the small conference room, if it was still available.

Better to get this over with before her mother and sister arrived. They would be watching her to see how she acted around Dylan and the image Alexis wanted to project was two old friends meeting again. Bygones were bygones. Fond memories, that sort of thing.

It sounded good, but when Alexis saw Dylan walking toward her in the lobby, she had no idea if she could pull it off.

"I'm sorry," he said at once, his face revealing signs of a sleepless night. "Not for kissing you—"

"You're not sorry you kissed me?"

"Heck no. That was great. Wouldn't have missed that. It was totally inappropriate and I know it. I regret that. But I'm apologizing for what I said." He gave her a somber look. "I wanted you to hate me."

"Good job."

"Yeah. I was trying to put it all on you, which was wrong." He flicked a hand through the air. "Well, I hold you in the highest esteem, it'll never happen again, etc. etc. Now, is Margaret going to be here soon?"

"Just like that? I'm supposed to forgive you and forget all about what a jerk you were just like that?"

"You want me to suffer? You got your wish. I have suffered. I'm suffering now. You know what I did? I drank and OD'ed."

"Dylan!"

"On milk and cookies. Lots and lots of cookies."

It did sound like something he would do.

Alexis snickered and then laughed, laughed until

her eyes watered and her sides hurt. She was still laughing when Margaret arrived. Even worse, she'd forgiven him.

"Now this is what I like to see," she said. "It's always easier when both sides get along." They headed for the conference room. "Especially when we have issues as serious as these."

Issues? "What issues?" Alexis had read the prenup. She hadn't discovered any issues.

They sat around the table. "Dylan has been a very naughty boy."

Both Dylan and Alexis stared at her. Did she know?

Margaret tapped the paper and sat back. "The conjugal-rights clause. Why, the way it's written, a judge could decide that Vincent could take a mistress, buy her a Harry Winston diamond ring the cost of which would come out of Alexis's settlement."

What? Alexis looked down at her own bare finger. She and Vincent were going ring shopping after they got back from Colorado.

Dylan grinned. "I wondered when you were going to catch that."

"How could you put that clause in?" Alexis asked.

When Dylan shrugged and didn't meet her eyes, she knew it had come from Vincent. Well, family law wasn't his strength. Thinking he knew everything about everything was.

Alexis sat back and listened to Dylan and Margaret hammer out new language. It was so effortless for Dylan.

She almost wished he hadn't apologized so she could still despise him. The fact was, she couldn't. She should have slapped his face. Or the verbal equivalent. And she sure shouldn't have kissed him.

He glanced over at her, including her in the conversation, but Alexis wasn't listening. One look from Dylan and the butterflies took off in her stomach.

A few kisses from Vincent and she saw ghosts in the bathroom.

Not a good sign. And she thought she handled stress well.

Margaret was smiling at her. "If that's everything, then I'll have fresh copies printed and we can sign after Vincent returns tomorrow."

"Thanks," Dylan said. "The facilities here aren't set up for that."

"My hotel has a full business center of which I've been gladly availing myself." She stood.

Alexis and Dylan stood, as well. "I do appreciate you flying out here. I'm sorry this has taken longer than we planned," Alexis said.

Margaret shook their hands. "It's been a pleasure. Ta ta, kiddies."

Alexis and Dylan glanced at each other as she left.

"That was pretty jaunty for old Margaret."

Alexis watched her lawyer hurry through the lobby. "She's met a man."

"Who?"

"Oh, I don't know. But only a man can put that kind of spring in a woman's step."

Dylan looked down at her. "So, Alexis, where's your spring?"

"Wyoming." They stood in the doorway looking out on the lobby. Alexis didn't quite know what to do with herself so she wandered toward the historical parlor.

Dylan followed. "He's coming back, isn't he?"

She wished Dylan would go away. Forgiveness was one thing. Attraction was another. "If he weren't coming back, he would have told me. Jilting isn't Vincent's style." Not on purpose anyway.

She stared up at the old photo of the girls of the house. This time she studied it, specifically Sunshine's face.

The girl who'd been talking to her was a dead ringer. So to speak.

"If you're at loose ends, would you like to take a walk around Maiden Falls? Maybe visit the falls themselves?"

It would be great to get out of the hotel. Alexis turned to Dylan, ready to accept, when the expression on his face stopped her.

Naked yearning. He wasn't even trying to hide it. No wonder he wasn't sorry he'd kissed her. He wanted to kiss her again. Worse, if he tried, she'd let him.

He might yearn, but he wasn't offering a concrete alternative to her current life's plan. Not that Alexis was interested. "I've got some puttering to do before my family gets here. Choose wines, check out the centerpieces for the wedding supper, that kind of thing."

"Alexis..."

Her breath hitched. He was going to say something he shouldn't. Maybe even offer her that alternative. "Don't."

"I was only going to say goodbye." Dylan reached

out and caressed her cheek with his knuckles. "If you change your mind, just say the word."

"And what word would that be?" she snapped.

"Walk. If you change your mind about going for a walk."

They gazed at each other for a long time. "I won't," she said at last.

With a tiny nod, Dylan strode from the room.

7

"HEY! WAKE UP!"

Sunshine blinked and forced her eyes all the way open. Rosebud stood over her.

"Sorry, I fell asleep on your couch. I know you like to read here."

"Never mind that," Rosebud said. "While you were sleeping, your groom took a powder."

"What?"

"He left."

Sunshine sat bolt upright. "Left as in *left?*"

Rosebud nodded. "He's gone."

"Where's Alexis?"

"She's still here wandering around and trying to avoid the cute one."

Sunshine winced. She felt hung over.

"What are you going to do?"

"Let me think." Thinking was hard. She needed a couple of years more sleep. Sunshine closed her eyes just to clarify her thoughts.

Rosebud poked her. "You appeared in front of someone other than your assigned couple, didn't you? That's why you're so tired," she whispered.

She needn't have bothered whispering. Miss Arlotta would still be able to hear her. "It was that Dylan, wasn't it? I can't believe you chanced it. I mean he's a good-looking one, but you only have to help this last couple and you'll get to go to the Eternal Picnic."

"It's okay. It was business. He's in love with Alexis and I'm afraid she's in love with him, too." Sunshine filled Rosebud in on last night.

Rosebud was nodding when Sunshine finished. "I think you're right."

Sunshine didn't want to hear that, especially from Rosebud, because Rosebud was very smart and very seldom wrong. "Why? What happened?"

"Only that they stood right here in this room and looked at each other making goo-goo eyes while their little hearts went pitter-patter. And now they're trying to avoid each other."

"Not that. It never works. Where are they?"

Rosebud took her hand. "In the ballroom." By the time she finished talking, they were there in time to see Dylan walk in on Alexis and the wedding coordinator.

"Ooh, feel those sparks."

Sunshine sighed. "Well, shoot patoot."

Rosebud patted her arm before drifting away. "If there's a wedding tomorrow, you'll deserve that trip to the Great Picnic."

Sunshine took in the expression on Dylan's face, the awkwardness, and the increasingly bleak look on Alexis's face.

The air was thick with sexual longing.

Ha. Now that was something Sunshine understood. Well, well. It appeared that Alexis had the right idea, but the wrong man. And it was up to Sunshine to help her figure it out.

Before tomorrow.

THE PIANO HAD BEEN MOVED in here and Dylan had thought the ballroom would be empty.

Once he'd decided to forget about a future with Alexis, he thought seeing her would be easier, not more difficult.

"I was looking for the piano," he explained.

"They moved it in here for tomorrow." Alexis stated the obvious.

Behind Alexis, Tracy was pouting at him because he hadn't called her. He'd forgotten all about Tracy.

"I was in town and found a book of Tin Pan Alley sheet-music reproductions." He held it up so Alexis wouldn't think he'd been stalking her.

"Go ahead." She gestured toward the piano. "You won't bother us."

But she would bother him.

Dylan sat down and turned to the table of contents. And there they were. Song titles from 1895–1920 that summed up his life right now: "I Can't Tell You Why I Love You But I Do." There it was in a nutshell, wasn't it? He wished he had time to figure out what he wanted to do.

"I've Got a Feeling for You" and he wondered how long it would last.

"I Love You in the Same Old Way." Maybe. Maybe not. Maybe it was a whole new way.

"Let Me Call You Sweetheart," except he had no right to call Alexis sweetheart anymore because he'd blown it seven years ago. Or had he blown it? Seven years ago, he'd been convinced that he'd made the right decision.

"Let Bygones Be Bygones." Alexis had forgiven him for last night far more quickly than he'd had any right to expect.

"I Just Can't Make My Eyes Behave." Dylan stole a look across the room where she was choosing between three centerpieces and taking a long time to do it. Centerpieces. Not legal maneuvers, but center-stupid-pieces. And they all looked alike. What was the big deal?

She was going to be miserable doing stuff like this for the rest of her life, couldn't she see that?

Alexis glanced at Dylan as though she felt him watching her. They stared at each other, then Dylan rippled a chord on the piano.

Pressing her lips together, Alexis turned back to Tracy, pointed at one of the centerpieces, then stood and hurried from the room.

And the song Dylan began to play? "Goodbye My Lady Love."

FORGETTING ABOUT DYLAN wasn't working. Vincent should never have left and he really shouldn't have fallen asleep last night.

And now she was only going to get three hours before her wedding to find out if they were compatible sexually.

Three hours, two of which she'd like to spend getting dressed and having her hair and makeup done, didn't leave much time. Not to mention her mother and sister hovering around—and she wanted them to—but how was she supposed to ask them to wait while she had a prewedding fling with the groom?

And if the spring was out of the fling, so to speak, then what? Was she prepared to walk away? Vincent would never postpone the wedding, especially for that reason. His pride wouldn't allow it. He'd cancel it outright and take the deal off the table.

The situation was awkward enough without Dylan hanging around reminding her what sexual compatibility was all about. If he weren't here, she could convince herself that sex wasn't all that important and buy into the idea that there were all kinds of ways to make love. Unfortunately, those ways didn't lead to children.

Alexis headed for the cellar to choose wines, wistfully wishing Vincent were there. She knew he was good at that, at least. She, on the other hand, had to rely on a list suggested by the sommelier.

The door leading to the cellar was at the top of thick stone steps. As Alexis descended, the air grew cooler. During prohibition, there had been a club hidden here and carriage lamps still shone dimly. She crossed an open area with attractive gray stone walls and ceiling, opened another door and was in the cellar proper. Bottles lined the walls and lay in racks in the middle of the room. It was like being in a library with wine bottles instead of books.

Alexis found a table made out of an old wine keg, along with three chairs, a light, wineglasses, corkscrew and an inventory book and guest book.

She was enjoying paging through the guest book and reading the comments from visitors all over the world when she heard other steps descending. That would undoubtedly be the chef, who had offered to change the sauce on the chicken to complement her choice of wines. And here she hadn't made a choice.

Alexis wanted to serve champagne with the salmon mousse and maybe add a few nibbles. Then there was the traditional white wine for the chicken and a red for the beef. And, since it was a special occasion, perhaps a dessert wine to go with the wedding cake and coffee. She couldn't help hoping Vincent would approve, then mentally edited her thought. She should hope Vincent would be pleased. She shouldn't have to constantly seek his approval. Honestly, she was going to have to change the dynamics in their relationship from underling assistant to full life partner. It was doubly hard because of the age difference. And Vincent would have to make an effort, too. Alexis had a suspicion convincing Vincent that he had to change in any way would be difficult.

The footsteps stopped and Alexis plastered a smile on her face for the chef, only to find Dylan standing there.

The smile left her face just as one formed on his. It would have been funny under other circumstances.

"I thought you were coming down here earlier," he said.

"No, earlier I chose centerpieces." And after all that, she couldn't remember which one she'd chosen. With Dylan sitting there playing the piano and staring at her, she'd been reminded of being caught wearing the naked negligee, which had reminded her of the expression on his face, which had contrasted so completely with Vincent's reaction, or more accurately nonreaction. With all this on her mind, she couldn't figure out what Tracy was telling her about the centerpieces, and why, if the other bride had already chosen them, Alexis had to choose them again. Something about dark purple and less silver. She didn't care. She honestly didn't care.

The more she tried to avoid Dylan, the more she found they were in the same place at the same time. With each chance encounter, it was like reliving the early days of their acquaintance when they'd already noticed each other, but hadn't yet become a couple.

It was a breathless anticipatory feeling and, darn it, she should not be feeling breathless and anticipatory.

"I thought I'd take a look around and pick a bottle of wine for dinner." He looked off to the side at the wines.

The sight of his profile brought back memories of when she used to awaken before he did and watch him sleeping next to her.

Would she ever, could she ever, feel that intense connection with someone again?

"Go ahead," Alexis told him as a door slammed. "That's probably the chef. He mentioned coming down here if the dining room wasn't too busy."

"It was packed when I saw it."

They fell silent, letting several moments pass before they realized that it was *too* silent.

Where were the footsteps?

Alexis stepped to the side. "Hello?"

No answer.

With a nervous smile at Dylan, she walked toward the entrance. "I don't see anyone," she called back.

"Well, I'll get on with it and get out of your way." Dylan looked around. "This is a lot of wine."

Alexis rejoined him. "Are you looking for a red or a white?"

"Red, I guess."

"I've got a list here." She showed him the printout of suggestions. "These are special, but not break-the-bank wines."

"Sounds like what I'm looking for. Where do we start?"

"I have a locator grid on this sheet." They both bent their heads over the paper. In the chilly air, Alexis could feel the heat from his body. "Let's head this way."

She and Dylan walked past dusty bottles.

"That's expensive-looking dust," Dylan said.

"Yes, it is. Keep walking." They laughed.

It was a self-conscious laughter, but the ice had been broken and Alexis relaxed.

"Look." She held up plastic-coated sheets of paper that hung from the racks. "Comments from people who ordered these wines."

"'Like drinking liquid sex,'" Dylan read. "Interesting choice of words."

"I'll say." Couldn't they ever get away from that topic?

"Here's one. 'Like sipping sunshine and swallowing shadows,'" Alexis read.

"What the heck does that mean?" Dylan asked.

"It means that someone had too much wine before he wrote that."

"What makes you think a man wrote it?"

"Because a woman would have used words like fruity and spicy and perfumed and good aftertaste."

"Not necessarily. Here we go. 'This is a good wine. It's not so expensive that I'm too worried about how I'm going to pay for it to enjoy it, but expensive enough that I won't be forgetting our anniversary again anytime soon.' Grinning, Dylan took a bottle from the wooden rack. "I've got my wine."

"I'd like to try that one, too." Alexis reached for a bottle, but Dylan spoke.

"Let's open mine and then you'll know what it tastes like. I can't drink this whole thing by myself. Well, I could, but after the cookies-and-milk incident, I'm taking it easy."

"You're a nut. Come on over here."

They returned to the wine-keg table and opened the wine with one of those fancy, European corkscrews.

Pouring a half glass each, Dylan said, "Now we've got to do this right. No chugging. Sniffing and swirling only."

Alexis chuckled.

Dylan put his nose in the glass.

"That's not your most attractive look."

He pulled back slightly. "Better?"

Alexis nodded and he inhaled. "Smells like wine!"

"All right!" They high-fived each other in mock celebration.

From the look on Dylan's face, Alexis guessed that

his hand was tingling as much as hers was. Abruptly, they each took a sip of wine.

Dylan nodded. "That's good. He's right. I wouldn't forget my anniversary after this."

Alexis was still hyperaware of him and had swallowed hers without tasting it. She tried again. "Oh. It's like drinking an Indian-summer sunset."

Dylan gave her an impressed look. "And you said women weren't poetic."

"I never drank a wine like this before." She'd shared wine at company dinners with Vincent, but had never enjoyed one more. "It's full and smooth and rich and...and mature. Wise." She'd never thought of wine as wise before. "It makes me content."

It was the wine she wanted for her wedding supper. She started to say as much, but stopped. How could she choose a wine she'd forever associate with Dylan for her wedding to Vincent?

She couldn't. "I'll put a star by this one on the list." And later she'd choose a different red. "Now for the whites."

"My cue." Dylan recorked his bottle and stood. "See ya." He took a couple of steps before turning back. "I do wish you well, Alexis. You know that, don't you?"

She shivered at the intensity in his eyes. Then she nodded and he disappeared behind the racks of wine. Alexis looked into her glass and breathed in the wine before slowly savoring the last swallows.

Okay. Time to regroup. She'd met an old flame who

had stirred up a few burning embers. It was time to let the fire go out. Because, to continue the fire analogy, Dylan had not offered any fuel.

And that was a very important point. She had no new options. During all the heavy looks and the stolen kisses, not once had he said something like, oh, "Break up with Vincent and marry me." Or even, "There's something here and we should explore it." Which, to be truthful, was awfully vague when it meant she'd have to cancel a wedding and most likely change jobs.

Was Dylan waiting for *her* to make the first move? If so, how unfair. He was the one who'd originally broken off with her. Was he waiting for her to break up with Vincent first? Also unfair.

She was so confused. It was a new feeling for her because Alexis never remembered being confused before. She was always able to examine the choices and information available to her and make a decision. If new relevant information came her way, then she reevaluated her position and either stuck with her original decision, or made a new one. There was never any of this dithering.

Okay. The fact was that Dylan was out of the picture. Whatever they had was in the past. She should focus on the future she'd planned and, while she was at it, choose a white wine.

There. She felt calmer and more sure of herself. And then she heard steps coming toward her. Dylan was back. "Alexis?" He exhaled and thunked the bottle on the table. "We're locked in."

"YOU LOCKED THEM IN THE CELLAR?" Rosebud rolled her eyes. "Couldn't you come up with something more original than that?"

Sunshine smiled knowingly. "Sometimes the oldies but goodies work best."

"YOU'RE KIDDING."

Dylan sat down and pulled the cork out of the bottle. "Check it out."

Alexis was already halfway to the entrance.

"And while you're pushing and pulling and pounding on the door, remember that we heard it slam," he called. "Remember the thick stone walls. Remember the outer room. Then come back here and have some more wine."

Alexis pulled the door handle. The door was so heavy it didn't even quiver. Nevertheless, she felt compelled to go through the motions of pounding and kicking on the door and calling out. "Is anyone in the other room?" she shouted.

Silence.

She went back to Dylan. He'd poured her another glass of wine. Full this time.

Well, it was a very good wine. She took a sip and then grinned at him triumphantly. "I have my cell phone with me. I'll call the hotel switchboard."

She pulled out her phone and started pressing the keypad. At that moment, the level of the battery-charge icon fell and the display light winked out. The phone was dead. "I can't believe it! I charged it last night."

"Not to worry." Dylan set down his glass and got out his own phone. "I'll just get the number from directory assistance first." He punched in the numbers and waited. "Yes. I'd like—hello? Hello?" He disconnected. "I hate dropped calls." He punched in the number again, then stared at his phone. After blinking at it a few moments he slipped it back into his pocket.

"What?"

Dylan sipped his wine then held it up to the light. "The battery is dead."

"Great." Alexis sat down. "At least I don't feel like such a dingbat."

"My phone had a full charge this morning and this was the first time I tried to use it today. Rotten luck that both phones decided to go wonky on us."

Alexis rubbed her hands together and sipped her wine. "It's beginning to feel chilly."

Dylan gave her a roguish look. "We can huddle together for body warmth."

"You know, I saw that coming." Alexis shook her head.

"If I hadn't said it, you would have been disappointed."

Alexis laughed and then, to her utter astonishment and subsequent embarrassment, she began to cry.

"Alexis." Dylan dragged his chair next to hers and drew her against his chest.

It felt so good, she cried harder. Where were these tears coming from?

"We're not going to be here long. Until dinner at the most," Dylan said soothingly. "Someone is bound to order wine sooner or later and they'll find us. Or your family will start asking questions and eventually the chef will remember that he'd offered to meet you here.

We might get a little hungry, but my gosh, we're not going to die of thirst."

Alexis laughed through her tears. "I'm sorry." She made a huge effort to pull herself together. "I'm not crying about that. I think I'm crying because you were always able to make me laugh."

"I understand perfectly."

He was lying. Smiling, she wiped her eyes as she pulled away. "No you don't." She sniffed.

"Have some wine. It's good for everything."

"You just don't like crying women. Don't worry. I don't, either."

"Are you okay?" His gaze searched hers.

"Oh, yeah. It's only that I haven't laughed in a while. Come to think of it, I haven't cried in a while, either. I've been sort of...focused? Disconnected from the world. That's it. You know what it's like to work and work and never watch television or read a book or see a movie and the only people you see are people who are working just as hard and are just as disconnected as you. Then your world becomes the work."

Dylan opened his arms. "You need a hug."

"Dylan."

"Okay, I need a hug."

"I thought you just needed wine."

"That, too. But I prefer a hug."

"Well, I need a comfortable chair." The metal ones were hard and cold.

"Here." Dylan patted his lap.

"Oh, right."

"Don't worry. You don't look like you've chunked up too much."

"You are incorrigible. But warm." Knowing she shouldn't and not caring a whole lot, Alexis walked around the little table and sat in Dylan's lap.

He wrapped his arms tightly around her and nudged her head against his shoulder with his chin. They sat silently for several minutes.

Dylan always gave good hugs. The strong and steady thump of his heart calmed her. If she moved her head a little, she could press her lips against the pulse in his neck as she used to.

Alexis, knowing no good would come of it, forced herself to imagine being comforted by Vincent. She couldn't. She flat-out couldn't. Not that Vincent was incapable of offering comfort, but she was wrapped in Dylan's arms right now.

"I know what it's like to work hard," he said quietly. "But I've never disconnected in the way you described. I won't allow it. Because, Alexis, no matter how much you give to the work, it'll never be enough. The work will always demand more. So I decide how many hours I'm going to work and I stop when I've put in those hours. Sure there are deadlines that require an extra push, but then I give myself time off afterward to recharge. If that means I'll never be the number-one family-law attorney in Texas or in Houston or even in my firm, then so be it."

"You make it sound so easy."

"It's not. I got yelled at a lot at first. But I was more efficient and at the end of a year, I'd accomplished a lot more than most. Are you burned out, Alexis? Is that it?"

She was burned out on relationships, not work. "Maybe."

"Have some wine."

He reached for a glass and her back felt cool where his arm had been. "Are you trying to get me drunk?"

"Good and relaxed. I want to talk about us seven years ago."

Alexis stiffened.

"See? Drink up. Concentrate on feeling wise and content."

Alexis let a mouthful of wine slip over her tongue. "It has a unique aftertaste. I wish I could identify it."

"Seven years ago—"

"Dylan, we don't have to talk about it."

"*We* aren't. *I* am."

She started to protest again, but his jaw was set. She was distracted by his jaw. In law school, it hadn't been quite so determined. Or so manly. She just stopped herself from tracing a finger along his chin.

Alexis's new fascination with his jaw escaped Dylan's notice. "We're both lucky enough to come from nice, normal families. Your parents put you through college, and my parents contributed what they could. But I come from Midwestern farming folks. There isn't a lot of spare cash in farming. A few of my relatives had a year or two at the junior college, but I was the first one to go away to school. I was the first one to graduate, let alone go on to law school. They were so proud. Second cousins and great aunts—relatives I hadn't ever heard of wrote me. I got cookies—"

"I remember! You always got care packages."

"I got more than that. They sent money. I never

asked and, as far as I know, neither did my parents. It was family supporting family. My great-aunt Ida sent me a thousand bucks. That must have been huge to her." He grinned. "Of course she's more than gotten it back in legal advice and courier fees. She goes to church on Sunday and spends the afternoon revising her will. I get a letter from her later in the week. I've got a template just for her."

"You're sweet." Alexis gave in to the urge to touch him and tapped him on the nose. Not very sexy, which was the point.

"I'm happy to do it. It's what I wanted to be able to do for my family. They gave me unconditional support. I didn't want to be a farmer and my dad just said to decide what I wanted to do and do it. So, after law school, I had to prove to all of them that their faith wasn't misplaced. I had a commitment to them. I couldn't make a commitment to you, too. I just flat-out wasn't ready."

A whole lot was now clear. "Why didn't you tell me this? Because I didn't let you," Alexis answered her own question. She'd been so hurt and so angry. She wouldn't accept his calls and avoided him for the rest of the semester. "But you could have shared how you felt obligated to your family. I mean, we went together for almost two years."

"Ah...you were a big-city girl."

"And you think I wouldn't have understood? Oh, come on. You can do better than that."

"Actually, I did talk about my family, but you weren't as fluent in guy talk then as you are now."

"Clearly." Obviously, she'd missed a huge indication of the way Dylan thought.

"Also you were making plans for after graduation and I noticed they were changing. There was a lot of 'we' talk. 'We have to figure out where we want to live so we can apply to firms in the same city.' That bothered me."

"It scared you."

"Okay, it scared me."

"Here, again, a conversation—"

"What did you think I was having with you that day?" He so rarely raised his voice. In the cellar, it sounded particularly loud.

"And I offered to go anywhere you wanted to go!" She could still remember it.

"I know." The jaw she thought was so manly now looked tense. "You had the opportunity to work for Gallagher Simmons in Austin and you were ready to turn them down for me."

"Yes. Because I loved you."

"I didn't want you to make that kind of sacrifice. You made me responsible for your future happiness. That's a horrible burden to put on anyone."

Had she?

"You were brilliant. You *are* brilliant. Everyone knew you would be a legal star. And here you were, ready to give it up for me."

"Not give it up," she protested.

"It sure sounded that way. I already had people depending on me. I couldn't handle anything more. And...it was just so bizarre to think that you'd make that kind of sacrifice for me. I couldn't..."

"I understand now." She pulled back. "I wish I didn't."

"Why?"

Alexis cupped his face with her hands. She hadn't had all that much wine, but it was cold and he was warm and she realized she'd spent seven years misjudging him. "Why? Because now that I understand, I know that you, my first love—if you don't count the one at thirteen, the one at fifteen, the two at sixteen, and the sorta one at seventeen, and the really not so good one at twenty—you, my first true love, are the best of the lot. I'm going to kiss you now."

His eyes flashed. "Is that a good idea?"

"Don't you think so?"

"I always think so, but the question I'm asking is will you hate yourself in the morning?"

"What morning? This is just a little make-up kiss."

Of course, if anyone thought she truly believed that, they'd be trying to sell her swampland somewhere.

Alexis settled her lips against his and it was like coming home. Unfortunately, it felt completely right.

Dylan kissed her back, but she knew he was keeping himself in check. Well, so was she. Which, she had to admit, became more and more difficult the longer they kissed.

"I hated feeling awful every time I thought of you," she murmured close to his mouth.

He exhaled. "It wasn't any easier for me, knowing you felt that way about me."

Smiling, Alexis lightly rubbed her lips against his. Technically, it wasn't kissing. Technically, it had much the same effect as kissing. She traced his jawline with her fingers, feeling the barest roughness. Dylan didn't have a heavy beard, which had meant lots of extended kissing sessions and no roughened mouth and chin. She inhaled his familiar scent and shifted on his lap.

"Alexis!" Dylan looked her in the eyes, then took her mouth in a hungry kiss. An inappropriate kiss. A kiss that was definitely headed somewhere it shouldn't.

She knew all the signs, one of which she was sitting on. And, in a bizarre way, she was reminded of Vincent's little problem, which would become her little problem when she married him.

Dylan had such a lovely big problem. She squirmed. What if, uh, Vincent's problem never grew into a big problem? Could she live with that, or without that, as the case might be? Because with Vincent in Wyoming until just before the wedding, how was she going to determine if there was a problem at all?

And speaking of problems...Dylan's tongue went unerringly to the sensitive place toward the side of the roof of her mouth and Alexis felt her control slipping. No other man had ever discovered that place and she'd never told them. Maybe she'd used it as a test. Or maybe she was afraid that on some subconscious level she'd be reminded of Dylan.

She broke the kiss and toyed with the knit collar of his shirt, pressing her lips against the side of his neck. "Did you ever do that with anyone else?"

He shook his head. "How could I?" he whispered. He drew his fingers along her cheek, and then he pulled her mouth back to his.

She shouldn't be kissing him, but the altitude must have thinned her resistance, like the way it had thinned the air.

Dylan's hands cupped her head as though he was afraid to move them to other parts of her body, but that didn't mean he didn't use his position to good advantage. His thumbs massaged her earlobes and the hollows just beneath them. His fingers teased the back of her neck. And his mouth...oh, that mouth.

Could she live without passion if she had to? Would she and Vincent ever develop such a sensual rapport?

What about Dylan? Could *he* live without passion—specifically passion with her? Or was she misjudging his level of interest?

At the point she couldn't stand any more, Alexis wrenched her mouth from Dylan's. "If you have anything to say, especially anything concerning the future, now would be an excellent time."

8

THERE WAS NOTHING LIKE forbidden lust. Dylan knew better then to kiss Alexis once more, but he was a man, after all. A man who, seconds before, had been in a lip lock with a woman he was probably still in love with. A woman who'd, understandably, just pointed out that he needed to state his intentions when all he'd intended was to kiss her for as long as possible.

Yep. That's what forbidden lust will get you.

He met her eyes squarely, knowing that what he said, what they said to each other in the next several minutes would be of life-defining importance. No pressure or anything.

Especially since he hadn't exactly figured everything out himself. This situation with Alexis had developed quickly—or had been seven years in the making, depending on which way he looked at it. He'd never expected to have her come back into his life again, and so had never thought of what he would do if fate gave him another chance.

The key was to figure out what Alexis wanted. Not what she said she wanted, but what she truly wanted. And whether it meshed with what Dylan wanted.

"A future with me would be different than a future with Vincent," he began carefully.

"It sure would." Alexis wiggled suggestively on his lap.

She was cheating.

"If you're waiting for an offer while you're still committed to Vincent, it ain't gonna happen." There were rules. Especially rules about the best man and the bride. Especially when the best man hoped to continue to practice law.

"What kind of offer are we talking?" The conversation had become a negotiation. Was he surprised? No. Did he like it? Also no.

Still, it was a valid question and she deserved an answer. Dylan took her hand, looking down at it as he ran his thumb over her knuckles. He was going to have to give her an answer at about the same time he figured it out for himself. Thinking back to the prenup, he said, "You want guarantees. Financial guarantees. I wouldn't offer that."

She laughed. "I wouldn't expect the same pre-nup from you as I would from Vincent."

But she would expect one. Okay, there it was. She'd never fully commit to the relationship knowing a pre-nup existed. Dylan gripped her hand and looked her right in the eyes. He didn't want her misunderstanding, especially since he thought this might be a deal breaker. "You couldn't expect any pre-nup from me."

She laughed again, but sobered quickly when he didn't even crack a smile. She pulled her hands away. "You're serious."

Slowly, he nodded. "Financially, we're pretty much on par. If I was advising a couple in similar circumstances, I would recommend keeping all personal property separate and establishing a joint account for purchases after the marriage. They'd both invest. They're both at risk."

Alexis presented her case. "Until the woman has children and can't bring in the same income. Then, she'd have to deplete her personal property to maintain the same level of contributions. And when she went back to work, she wouldn't be earning as much, because she'd have lost tenure and experience during the time she took off to care for the children. In the meantime, her partner would very likely have received salary increases and perhaps a promotion. They'd no longer be at parity. And should said partner become bored and want to divorce, the woman would have taken a financial hit, while the man would not. A pre-nup would address that."

"The man," Dylan rebutted, "assuming traditional division of parenting duties, would not expect the woman to continue to contribute financially if she was no longer employed. Neither would he be able to increase his personal property because he would have to make up for the lack of financial contributions from the woman."

"But his ability to make more money would be enhanced by the fact that he hadn't had an interruption in his employment history," she argued.

"And I think the marriage should start out on faith."

"Ha!" She looked at him in amazement. "Ha!" she repeated. "That's because you're the man. You don't have as much at risk."

"I can concede some of the financial question."

"Some?"

"A lot." He stopped short of saying money wasn't everything. "Traditionally, in case of divorce, most custodial parents are women. The man suffers by being separated from his children."

"He gets to see them on weekends for fun. The mother has to discipline them and make sure they do their homework and get to school on time. She's the no-fun parent. The dad is fun and games and usually has more money for those fun and games. It takes a really strange kid to appreciate that. And let's not get into child-care expenses."

"Let's not because the dad would be paying child support."

"Which is never enough."

Dylan drew a calming breath, a deliberate attempt to slow down the rapid exchange. "There are no guarantees, Alexis. We're arguing about something that only happens in a worst-case scenario."

"Isn't that what you do for a living? Make legal plans for worst-case scenarios?"

"Usually, it's a second marriage where one or both partners has children whose inheritance they want protected. Or the bride and groom have vastly different financial profiles. Or, increasingly, partners in a business want the business protected from upheaval in the event one of them divorces. In the absence of those considerations, sometimes you've got to take a chance."

"I just want to make sure that the man is taking the same chance."

She wasn't going to give an inch. Well, neither was

he. Alexis was so concerned about preserving herself that she was missing the whole point of marriage—two people forming one unit, one life partnership.

He understood her marriage to Vincent, now. She didn't love him, so she wasn't going to invest herself emotionally. And with all the financial worries taken care of, she wouldn't have to invest herself financially, either.

No, the only thing she was selling was her soul. And she didn't even know it. But that was another issue.

Dylan verbally laid his cards on the table. "My wife and I won't have a pre-nup."

"My husband and I will," Alexis countered at once.

And there it was. No room for compromise. To have a future together, one of them would have to give in. The only hope they had was if one of them changed her mind.

Alexis searched his eyes, then stood. Dylan wanted to rub his legs, but didn't.

"Well," she said, "I'm glad we had this chat. It clarified things. And I have to say that I'm surprised at your position on pre-nups."

"They're necessary in some circumstances but not for the couple we discussed." He gave her a half smile. "Besides I believe in the magic of love."

"Oh, please."

"I don't know what else to call it. All I know is I've seen starry-eyed couples come in to discuss the pre-nup and afterward, something is missing. The magic is gone."

"It's called a reality check. They get the same look when they buy insurance or draw up their wills."

"You're so tough. So cynical," he said.

"So realistic."

So wrong. But he didn't say so aloud.

At least he'd had a shot.

He wondered what she was feeling. Probably nothing. He on the other hand...was going to think about it later.

Alexis wandered over to the other chair and sat down. To cover the awkwardness, Dylan began flipping through the guest book. The front pages covered the history of the inn and the wine cellar, particularly the club during the Prohibition era. He began reading aloud about the thickness of the walls and some of the people reputed to have frequented the club. "And no one was ever caught," he read, "because of the secret back door."

"What?"

"No one was ever caught because the patrons escaped through the wine cellar to the secret back door." They stared at each other.

"Do you suppose that secret back door is still here?" she asked.

"Let's look for it."

Dylan was glad to have something to distance them from their earlier discussion and figured Alexis was, too. They started on the opposite wall from the door and felt their way around the perimeter. Nothing.

"I suppose they boarded it up." Alexis stamped her feet.

Dylan was getting chilly, himself. "Then we should see the boards." He ran his fingers over the stones and mortar. No cracks. Nothing.

The back wall was topped with red bricks above three giant wine barrels. He stood back and squinted, trying to see if there were any changes in color in the bricks that might signal a more recent remodel. Again, nothing.

"You know, it said 'secret', so that means it's hard to find, but it can't be so hard to find that people couldn't leave in a hurry." Alexis had walked back to the guest book.

"They could have just covered it up."

"I don't get the impression much was changed down here. Hey, there was a winery in town. That explains where those oak casks came from. Oh, my gosh. Look how they cleaned them." She held up the book.

Dylan went over and saw old black-and-white photos of a man going through something that looked like a pet door. "They scrubbed them down from inside?"

"I guess they had to clean them somehow."

Dylan turned back and studied the three large casks. After walking over to them he looked at the small square doors and tried to imagine fitting through one. "Man, you put on a few pounds and there goes the job, unless you could convince your boss to cut a bigger door."

Alexis looked up. "Dylan..."

A bigger door. "I'm with you." He'd bet these barrels weren't just decorative.

Dylan waited until Alexis made her way over to the giant casks before asking, "Which one hides the door?"

"My guess is the middle one. If it were the ones to

either the left or the right, it would be too hard to remember, especially if you were slightly tipsy."

"Works for me." He and Alexis studied the edge of the middle cask. They tried pulling and pushing, but had no luck. Dylan got one of the chairs and stood on it, examining the hoops for hinges.

"Try the other side," Alexis suggested.

"That would make it open backward."

"And harder to find."

Dylan moved the chair, stood on it and immediately found a set of hinges. "I don't believe it. Right or left is too difficult to remember, but a backward door isn't?"

It took both of them to get the door open enough for them to squeeze into the dark confines of the wine barrel. There was a musty, oaky, but not unpleasant smell.

"Can you see anything?" Alexis asked.

Dylan removed his key ring and pressed the vanity light on his car-alarm transmitter. The back of the cask was missing and a door was in the wall.

"This is kind of exciting," Alexis said. "An adventure."

"Glad you're having a good time. Have you noticed how blasted cold it is in here?"

"Well, yes. But I didn't say anything because I didn't want you to think I was whining."

"No. It's become a lot colder. Was a front supposed to come through? Did you check the weather forecast for tomorrow?"

"Cool and sunny."

Dylan reached for the door handle. "This thing feels frozen. Okay, get ready to pull."

He and Alexis both worked their hands together on the big metal ring and yanked. The door fell open easier than they expected and sent them stumbling backward as something that had been pressing against it fell inwards.

"Is that dirt?" Alexis asked.

Dylan pressed his tiny light, which illuminated a hill of white.

Snow.

"That can't be snow," Alexis said.

"It's white. It's cold. It's wet. What else could it be?"

"I don't know. Maybe this leads to a meat locker that needs to be defrosted. There can't be this much snow. It's May. My wedding."

Dylan climbed up the drift and began digging. His hands, warm Southern hands, went numb almost at once. A muffled howling grew louder.

"What's that?" Alexis asked.

"I don't know." It sounded like a wild hungry animal, but he chose not to share that with her.

"Can you see daylight?"

"I see dark."

"As in evening dark?"

Dylan was silent for a moment, his brain trying to process what he saw. He suddenly had a memory from his Midwestern farm childhood. "It's blizzard dark."

"What's that?" Alexis had grown up in south Texas. She hadn't seen much snow.

"It's snowing so hard it's dark."

"You're kidding."

Dylan slid back down the snowdrift and marched

over to her. "Say something so I know where you are."

"Dylan?"

Smiling grimly to himself, he cupped his icy hands around her neck.

She squealed.

"Yeah. It's cold. Too cold to joke. Now, I'm going to shine this puny little light over there and you're going to climb that snow mountain and go through the opening at the top of the doorway. And you're going to hurry."

Dylan's fingers were so numb he had a difficult time pressing the button. Alexis was already climbing up the snow, laughing all the way.

Ho. Ho. Ho.

He was glad somebody was having a good time.

They emerged outside into a moaning wind and snowflakes that felt like pieces of ice against their faces, which, to be sure, they were.

"Where are we?" Alexis shouted.

"Who knows. Someplace hidden from the entrance to the old house." He pushed her forward. "Go that way and keep touching the wall so we don't wander away from the inn."

"Is this the way back inside?"

"I don't know, but if we stand here arguing about it, we'll freeze."

Dylan couldn't remember ever being this cold. Just a few hours ago, he'd been walking the quaint touristy streets of Maiden Falls. Now, he was trudging through an icy wilderness, fighting for his life.

Alexis was doing a pretty good job of fighting for

her own life. In fact, she was leading. He should be leading. He was the man. But she made a most excellent windbreak.

"I found a window," she shouted.

Dylan was tempted to break it, but they had nothing to break it with except their shoes and all he needed was frostbitten toes to go with his frostbitten hands.

Alexis apparently had no fear of frostbite because she'd already removed her shoe and was pounding on the window.

Even if she succeeded in breaking the double-paned thermal glass, how did she think she was going to get inside?

In fact, the pounding attracted the attention of someone inside who motioned for them to keep walking. Ten feet away was the door. It was snowing so hard, they'd been unable to see it.

They stumbled inside and found themselves in the mudroom outside the kitchen.

"Come in, come in!" One of the staff said, then shouted for someone to get blankets.

Dylan and Alexis were led toward the ovens where they stood and dripped, probably breaking all sorts of health codes, until someone from housekeeping brought a mountain of blankets that they wrapped themselves in.

In the meantime, the chef hurried over to Alexis. "I could not find you earlier."

"I—I was locked in the cellar."

The man actually paled. "But how did you get out?"

"We read about the secret door during Prohibition

and looked until we found it," she told him. "It led outside, but there was this snow."

He threw up his hands. "This storm is unbelievable. I am making good old-fashioned chicken soup for tonight. Would you two like a bowl now?"

Alexis and Dylan nodded and sat at a long stainless-steel prep table. The chef, himself, brought them bowls of soup. Dylan thought he might just be able to make his fingers work now.

"I know it sometimes snows in May," someone remarked, "but nothing like this. I hope no one else is trapped outside."

"And the news hasn't made any special mention of it, so it must be very localized," added another of the kitchen staff.

"One thing, no one is getting in or out tonight," the chef said.

"What about tomorrow?" Alexis paused with the spoon halfway to her mouth. "Vincent! And my wedding!"

The chef seemed unconcerned. "The hotel has snowblowers or you can move the ceremony to the ballroom."

"Oh, Tracy and the union guys will love that," Alexis muttered.

Personally, Dylan thought the wedding location wasn't as much of a problem as the lack of a groom, but who was he to point that out? Well, the best man, but still he was going to stay out of it and eat his soup.

They shivered and gobbled soup for the next several minutes as the chef and his staff worked around them.

"I feel so much better. Thank you." Alexis carried her bowl over to the sink.

Dylan figured he'd better go, too. The staff was already deep into dinner preparations and they were only in the way. "Thanks." He saluted the chef and followed Alexis out of the kitchen.

They both looked like taupe mummies in their blankets, but Dylan was the last person to care. "You never finished choosing your wines," he said. "Want to change clothes and meet back down there?" He grinned so she'd know he was kidding.

"Very funny. I'm headed for a nice hot bath." She punched the elevator button and leaned against the wall. Even tired, she had her guard up. Those dark eyes of hers told him nothing.

"I might go for cognac or brandy or something that'll burn its way down my throat and *then* go for the hot bath," Dylan told her.

"Thanks for getting me out of there," she said.

"You had just as much to do with it. Are you going to be okay?"

"Sure. It wasn't like we were stranded on a mountain, or anything."

Mechanical sounds from the shaft announced the arrival of her elevator. Just as well. Her hair had been damp and had dried naturally into wild curling wisps that made her look more approachable than she'd been all weekend. And, in spite of the finality of their earlier conversation, Dylan definitely wanted to approach. He supposed he'd always feel that way about her.

But the only thing Dylan was entitled to approach

was a bottle of something in the bar. "See you tomorrow."

She gave him a tired nod and he watched as the elevator doors closed. He trailed his blanket as he squished his way to the bar, then sat down and ordered a double.

"A double what?" asked the bartender.

"I've been out in the storm and tomorrow I'm going to be the best man, not the groom—important distinction—best man at the wedding of the woman who might just be the love of my life. Give me a double of whatever you think I need."

The bartender stared at him, then poured an amber liquid into a brandy snifter. "On the house, man."

Dylan raised it to the bartender. "Thank you." When he sipped, he felt the warmth all the way down to his stomach. His stomach didn't need warming. The soup had taken care of that. His heart needed warming, but Dylan had a feeling it was going to be a long, long time before he recovered from this weekend.

The thing of it was, he wouldn't compromise on the pre-nup issue for one important reason. It represented a basic lack of trust on Alexis's part and an unwillingness to fully commit to a marriage. She wanted to hold something of herself in reserve. She wanted an escape hatch.

In Dylan's mind, a person was either committed, or not. Anything less was setting the marriage up for failure.

He swirled the liquid in the snifter and took another sip. He didn't know why she felt this way. Her parents were still married, so he guessed she'd been hurt by somebody. Maybe several somebodies.

He stared into the glass thinking he was probably one of those somebodies. What irony. Before, she was willing to commit too much, now not enough. She was protecting herself, that's what she was doing.

Dylan sat up. He hadn't convinced her that she could trust him. That was the trouble. And had he told her he loved her? No, because he hadn't known himself. He should go do that. He should go do that right now.

"Bartender, I'd like another one of these to go." He signed his room number and with a sense of urgency he didn't understand, and took both balloon glasses upstairs to Alexis's room.

"Vhat is viz all zee shouting? You know he cannot hear you."

"Hello, Countess," Sunshine croaked from her seat at the bar. "I was hoping he could sense something. I think he finally did. He's on his way upstairs and he's got two glasses."

"Mebbe he just vants to get drunk."

"No, I think he's going to see Alexis."

"So zee shouting is finished? Good. You vere disturbing our poker game." The Countess swept the train of her robe out of the way and stalked back to the parlor.

After mimicking the Countess's regal strut behind her back, Rosebud drifted in. "You might have overdone it on the snow. You nearly froze them to death."

"I didn't want that other man coming back."

"No problem. Nobody is coming or going."

"Good." Sunshine beamed. "And now, Rosebud, come and see what I can do with bubbles."

"Mom?" At the sound of her mother's voice, Alexis gripped the cell phone tightly. She could use a good motherly hug right about now. "What room are you in?"

"We're stuck in Denver. You're snowed in."

"You mean, you mean you aren't here?"

Patty O'Hara's voice assumed a calm tone mothers of brides had been using for centuries. "That's right, we're in Denver."

"But...but..."

"Honey, these people know how to deal with snow. They'll have the roads plowed by tomorrow and we'll be able to get there in plenty of time for the wedding." Her mother may have been overdoing the calm.

Alexis should try some herself. "Oh. Great." Even to her ears, she sounded less than convincing.

"Oh, honey. I wish I could be there with you now, but you'll be fine. Take a long warm bath and go to bed early and tomorrow will be here before you know it."

That's what she was afraid of. "Okay. Good night, Mom. Drive safely tomorrow."

Alexis just couldn't tell her mother everything that had happened—and she wasn't talking about getting locked in the cellar and the trudge through the white wilderness. No, she was talking about her little conversation with Dylan.

Why bring it up? Nothing had happened. In spite of

all the talk, everything was the same, except she was a little colder. That, she could fix.

Alexis had filled the claw-footed tub with bubbles and she intended to soak until she was a prune. She lit the candles she'd been going to use with Vincent and got into the tub. The water was scaldingly hot but she eased herself down and felt immediately better. She loved the shape of the tub. It was huge, but deep and curved in a way that allowed her to rest her head back.

She felt as though she were in an ad for bath products, except she needed longer hair so she could sweep it up and let a few sexy tendrils escape. Instead, her hair was one giant tendril. Fine. She couldn't see the mirror from the bathtub, anyway.

Tension seeped from her, but irritation remained. Dylan, the King of Pre-nups, didn't intend to have one for himself. Was that hypocritical, or what?

Not only that, he expected her to break off with Vincent this weekend before he'd discuss a future with her.

Okay. He had a point there, but not one she liked. Maybe if he'd given her a hint...No. If she really felt that tempted by anything Dylan might offer, she should break it off with Vincent right now.

Except she had never pretended to love Vincent. So, basically, she was tempted by different things.

No. There was no tempting. Vincent was her future. Dylan was her past.

The door to the bathroom slowly opened, letting out all the lovely warm air. Great. The lock must not have caught. Alexis didn't want to get out of the tub, so she scooted forward and stretched her leg toward the door. Just a little further and she could kick it shut.

"Alexis?"

It sounded as though her past was calling her.

"Alexis?" There was alarm in Dylan's voice and she could hear him coming closer.

He was in her room? How did he get into her room?

"Alexis? Are you okay?"

"Dylan! Don't come in—"

But he was already at the door of the bathroom. The open door of the bathroom. And there she was with her leg stuck in the air. She pulled it back into the tub. "I'm taking a bath," she pointed out when he didn't immediately leave.

Dylan stepped inside. "You scared me. I came by and your door was open." He exhaled and handed her one of the two brandy snifters he carried. "I brought you something warming." He took a sip from his glass. "I can't believe you're in the tub with the door wide open."

And she couldn't believe he was still in her bathroom. "It just came open!"

"I'm talking about your room door. When I got here, it was standing open. You should be more careful. Anyone could wander in."

Alexis sank lower into the bubbles. "Anyone did." She looked up at him and watched the expressions flit across his face until his eyes widened slightly and she knew he'd just realized that she was in the tub and that there was nothing between them but a bunch of rapidly popping bubbles.

9

AND SPEAKING OF BUBBLES...Alexis felt a draft and followed Dylan's gaze in time to see a thin layer of those bubbles becoming rapidly thinner.

Due to its location, Alexis wanted that particular layer to stay especially thick. She mounded some bubbles from near her shoulder and poofed them downstream. But darn it, there went another layer. She looked up at Dylan in suspicion, but, though he was breathing heavily, it wasn't concentrated enough to move bubbles around.

"I'm getting cold," she complained.

"Sorry." He shut the door.

And he was still on the inside.

"Uh..." Not that she was a particular prude, and it wasn't as though he hadn't seen everything before, but...

"Drink your brandy. Or cognac. Or whatever it is."

"You don't know?"

"I know it's good."

Trying to remain nonchalant about him standing there, she took a sip. "It's very...strong."

"It'll grow on you. You'll feel so warm and relaxed you'll forget all about how cold we were in the cellar."

Speaking of cold, there had to be a draft in here because she was having the most difficult time trying to keep her bubbles arranged, especially when the amount of bubbles decreased by the second. She scooted farther down in the tub. "I appreciate the drink," she said to encourage him to leave. "It was thoughtful when I know you're eager to get into your own bath."

Dylan didn't take the hint. Swirling the liquid in the brandy snifter, he wasn't even making eye contact.

No, he was watching as islands of bubbles formed where once there had been great continents.

Beneath the surface of the water, Alexis made little wave motions with her free hand. Must keep Antarctica down south where it belonged.

"I don't have a claw-footed tub in my bathroom." His eyes still watched the bubbles and Alexis still tried to pretend she was casual about him being in the bathroom.

"You must be in the new building, then."

Dylan nodded absently, still swirling and sipping his drink. What was this stuff? She tasted it. Not bad. Dylan was right, the more she drank, the better it got. She should be able to identify it.

In her preoccupation, Alexis momentarily forgot about the arrangement—or lack of arrangement—of the bubbles.

Dylan's fixed stare alerted her. Looking down at herself, she saw that she was much higher in the water than she'd been. She scooted down, the resulting wave action lapping dangerously against her breasts.

She squinted at the bubbles, now not nearly so opaque as they'd been.

The time for subtlety was at an end. "Dylan, I think you'd better—"

"Join you? I thought you'd never ask." He set his glass on the floor by the tub and dropped his blanket.

Alarmed—no, not alarmed. Thrilled more like, but she should have been alarmed. So, alarmed, Alexis protested as Dylan kicked off his sodden shoes. "I didn't ask you!"

Wearing a strange smile, and, at least for now, all his clothes, Dylan emptied his pockets. Cell phone, keys and wallet ended up in a pile on the bathroom counter.

"Dylan, you can't..."

"Say it with more conviction, Alexis."

She drew a deep breath—not such a good idea—then let it all out in a whoosh when Dylan ripped off his socks and belt, then stepped into the tub, fully dressed.

"What are you doing?"

"Getting warm. Getting relaxed. Getting lucky?"

"Not on your life."

He laughed. "Scoot forward."

She hunched forward covering her breasts. "Dylan. Get out of the bathtub."

He stopped. "Do you truly want me to get out of the bathtub, or are you protesting because you think you should?"

"Evil man."

Chuckling evilly he slid down behind her.

"Dylan, water is sloshing over the sides." And taking bubbles with it.

"The blanket will absorb it. And I'll clean up any

leftover mess. Relax." He pulled her back against him and wrapped his arms around her.

Relax? He was kidding, right? If anyone had told her a week ago that she'd be sharing a bathtub with Dylan Greene, she wouldn't have believed it. She barely believed it now. It felt so good. So intimate. So incredibly weird.

"Uh, Dylan?"

"Hmm?" He rested his chin on her head.

"What's with the clothes?"

"Plausible deniability."

"Excuse me?"

"It would be inappropriate for me to be naked in the bathtub with you while you're engaged to someone else."

"Inapprop—! *I'm* naked!"

"I noticed that. But I try not to judge people by my own high moral standards."

She tried to jab an elbow into his stomach, but he'd laughingly anticipated such a thing and only gripped her tighter.

Alexis gave up and let herself go limp against him. He promptly kissed the side of her neck, but with such gentle tenderness, she couldn't protest. She'd missed this. She'd missed this so much. Her body responded to him almost automatically. For a long time, it had responded to the *idea* of Dylan.

He kissed her again and beneath the water, her breasts tightened.

"Dylan." She sighed. "What are you doing?"

"Reminding you about us."

"'Us' was over a long time ago."

He was silent for a moment as his fingers idly moved back and forth against her arms. "I'm thinking it's still there. It's just been hibernating."

"No," she said. "I'm pretty sure that 'us' suffered a fatal blow that day."

"Nope. A coma. And now, it's awake."

"If that's the way you want to look at it, fine. But things have changed. I've changed. I don't even know if you've changed or not. Don't you see, Dylan?"

He reached over the side of the tub and handed her the snifter. "Close your eyes and I'll tell you what I see. I see the same Alexis I fell in love with. She's had experiences I haven't shared, but the woman who always picks the red onions out of her salad is still the same."

"I can't believe you remember that."

"You still pick them out?"

"Yeah." Alexis smiled and sipped the...it must be cognac. She'd only tasted it on one other occasion when the lawyers she was with—Vincent and his contemporaries—had been having cigars and cognac. She couldn't manage a cigar, so she'd accepted the cognac. It tasted a lot better without the cigar smoke.

Dylan began to talk and Alexis soaked and listened, feeling the vibrations in his chest.

"I fell in love with a young woman who liked cuddling, who made me smile, and made me think. Who made me a better person because I wanted to be worthy of her. I loved a bright, ambitious young woman who could defend any position, right or wrong. A young woman who could remove her emotions and think logically. You're still that woman, aren't you, Alexis?"

"Basically."

"I advise clients to try thinking with their heads instead of their hearts. But you know, sometimes thinking with the heart is best after all."

"My heart has been shattered one too many times. It's retired from thinking."

"When it did think, what did it think about me?"

"Before or after the breakup?"

"Before."

"It thought you were an idealist. It wanted some of that idealism, because...because I may be too cynical."

"Gullible. I was often gullible."

That gullibility had been a large part of his appeal. "But you could always dissect conflicts."

"But didn't have the guts to follow through. You did."

"We were a good team."

"We can be a good team again."

Dylan had been very clever. He'd positioned himself behind her so she couldn't see his eyes. Deliberately, she'd bet. It forced her to listen to his words—which still hadn't offered anything concrete. "Are you suggesting we become a team again?"

There was a silence. "No suggestions until you're free."

Alexis absolutely was not interested in a few weeks of fun and games. Not that she had anything against fun and games, but not now. Not when she'd planned her life. She had to know if he was offering more. "I'm not trading away a good thing until I know what's behind door number two."

"Would you be trading away a good thing?"

"You're familiar with the pre-nup."

Dylan shifted and Alexis felt his hands move away from neutral territory into decidedly unneutral territory. "It's the after-nup I'm asking about."

"What do you mean?"

Dylan didn't reply. His hands were doing all the talking. He ran them down the sides of her body as far as he could reach.

The little surge of pleasure was unexpected and she gasped. "What are you doing?"

"Showing you what's behind door number two."

His hands stroked and slid and slipped against her hips and thighs. That was enough door number two for her. So it would just be fun and games. Prime fun and games, but she was going to have to pass. She leaned forward, preparing to get out of the bathtub when Dylan kissed the back of her neck.

He'd remembered how he could make her weak by kissing the back of her neck.

Not fair.

She'd actually dated men who'd never kissed the back of her neck. When she'd tried to show one, to let him know that it was an erotic hot spot for her, he'd only squeezed her breasts harder.

She sighed and knew Dylan heard. With his tongue, he traced ever widening circles across her neck until she was boneless with desire. Honestly, she was so easy. Vincent, if he made any sort of effort at all, should not have any compl—

Vincent. Gritting her teeth, Alexis prepared to wrest her neck away from Dylan's mouth.

"I never appreciated how responsive you were," he murmured.

"And I, ah, never appreciated how you gave me the chance to respond."

"My pleasure." He immediately upped the stakes with nibbling.

Alexis hadn't found a good nibbler in a long time. She forgot about leaving and arched her neck to give Dylan access to as much of it as he could reach.

Speaking of giving access...Alexis looked down, noting that the bubbles were more of a lacy veil now, and clearly saw Dylan's hands very quietly resting on her hipbones when they could have been enhancing the whole experience. Now *he* could squeeze her breasts and she wouldn't complain at all.

Dylan reached her earlobe and sucked on it gently before nipping it with his lips. Okay, so his nipping didn't need a lot of enhancement. In fact, too much enhancement might prove explosive.

Oh, goody.

As Dylan moved from one ear to the other, Alexis took his hands and tried to bring them to her breasts.

"Uh-uh." He rested his hands lightly on her shoulders and the only enhancement she got was from a few measly trickles of water that dripped down her chest.

"What's wrong?"

"No naughty touching."

"Are you insane?"

"Getting that way."

"I don't understand."

"You just get to see what's behind door number two. You don't get to go through door number two."

"Why not? I'm thinking door number two is feeling really good."

"Excellent. But you have to give up the key to door number one."

"You're trying to seduce me away from Vincent?"

"I prefer to think of it as refreshing your memory."

"In that case, my memory needs more refreshing." Alexis tried to turn around in the tub to kiss him properly, but he wouldn't allow it.

"Dylan!"

"I'm still wearing all my clothes and all I've done is kiss your neck. My conscience is clear." He nuzzled her neck. "How's yours?"

He was so...so smug. Sexy, but smug. It made her determined not to give in.

But if *he* gave in...

"If my conscience is going to feel guilty, it needs a lot more to feel guilty about." She deliberately wiggled her hips against his and a very significant lump. She danced her fingers down its length. Glad to know she wasn't alone in this.

"Yes, I'm aroused. That shouldn't surprise you. Neither does it change anything."

However, she did notice his nuzzles weren't quite as tender or gentle as they'd been. In fact, there was an urgency about them that hadn't been there in the past few minutes.

Alexis threw a few soft moans into the mix and tried

to move his hands again. They were gripping her shoulders pretty hard.

They slid down her arms and she smiled in both triumph and anticipation.

But Dylan dipped his hands into the water and swept the remaining colonies of bubbles toward her. There were just enough left to mound in his hands. Still smiling, Alexis closed her eyes. She felt the bubbles tickle her breasts, then nothing more.

She opened her eyes to find that Dylan was using the bubbles to avoid touching her.

She reached out and both his hands and the bubbles disappeared. A genuine moan of frustration escaped.

"Be good and the bubbles come back."

"I want more than bubbles," she complained.

Dylan kissed her neck, apparently the only place he'd allow himself to kiss her. "I'm not going to touch you, but that doesn't mean you can't touch yourself."

What a lovely idea. Men loved it when they watched women touch themselves. Men went wild when women touched themselves.

Dylan was going to regret giving her the idea.

"Oh, thank you," she said in a deliberately husky voice.

Throwing back her head so Dylan would have a good view, she massaged her breasts, making sure she lifted them out of the water, making sure he saw how wet and slick and close to his mouth they were.

Dylan's breathing changed, but so did hers as she imagined the desire in his eyes.

"More. You want more," he urged her. He used his tongue to trace circles on her neck, which Alexis imitated with her thumbs until she'd made two taut peaks.

Surely now Dylan would give in.

She moaned and stretched her arms over her head, then tried to flip over but Dylan clamped his legs around her.

Okay. Fine. Let him resist *this*.

Alexis brought her arms down, panting just a little as she ran her hands over her breasts and continued under the water until she slid them behind her to the juncture of Dylan's legs.

She'd no sooner clamped her fingers around him than he pulled her hand away. "That's just a little bit too naughty, wouldn't you say?"

The man had to be made of iron. One part of him was, anyway.

Time for the heavy artillery.

Alexis let her head lean back, which not only gave Dylan access to more of her neck, but allowed him to see her hands slither southward right under Antarctica.

Alexis let her legs fall open and her fingers headed through her curls right for the sweet spot.

Dylan was behind her, breathing heavily.

Alexis touched herself and gave a convincing shudder as she imagined Dylan's reaction. The next shudder wasn't quite as artificial and the one after that, well, not at all, actually.

She forgot that she was playing a game of who-can-hold-out-the-longest with Dylan and got caught up in her own pleasure.

"Yes," he whispered and kissed her neck.

"You've been kissing that one spot for several minutes. If you're not careful you'll give me a hickey. Now, Dylan, there are a lot of other places you can kiss. And lick. And touch."

"Shall I show you what I'd like to do?"

She'd won! Of course, in this game, there were no losers. "Yes, please."

Dylan moved his hands down her arms and Alexis actually quivered.

The water had cooled but she felt hot and buoyant.

Dylan took hold of her left wrist and guided that hand back to her breasts. At the same time he placed his fingers over her right hand and set up a sensuous rhythm down there.

"This is what I would do," he whispered.

The rat still wasn't touching her, but Alexis forgot to protest.

"I would start moving slowly and listen to your breathing, waiting for it to quicken."

Alexis bit her lip in an effort to keep from breathing faster, but couldn't.

"Then I'd give your breasts some more attention." He tugged on her right hand.

"No!" Alexis protested. This was not the time to move her right hand.

"One hand then." Dylan manipulated her fingers over her breasts while simultaneously increasing the rhythm of her other hand.

And then Alexis stopped analyzing, stopped trying to win any stupid games and surrendered to the incredibly erotic feeling of Dylan's hands over hers.

The only sound in the bathroom was the lapping of

the water and Dylan's whispers as he continued to describe his actions in detail.

"Your skin is slick and smooth and hot. *You* are slick and smooth and hot."

Alexis moved her hips against their joined hands. A gasp escaped, then another and then, incredibly, she felt the pressure begin to build.

No way. Without Dylan touching her? With just the sound of his voice and a few kisses on her neck?

Apparently so.

And apparently...right...now.

She surged against their hands, her head moving from side to side.

Water sloshed over the side of the tub. Water got in her ears. Her head collided with Dylan's chin and he probably got squashed against the side of the tub, but Alexis didn't care.

Pleasure rippled through her, unexpected but welcome. Really, really welcome.

She went limp against Dylan as the surface of the water lapped against her shoulders, calming about the same time she did. She laced her fingers through Dylan's.

His lips moved against the side of her neck just beneath her ear. "And that is what I'd do if I were to touch you."

He just had to say it. The water seemed much cooler all of a sudden. "Obviously I can do a fine job by myself."

"You had expert direction." He shifted. "And now, I'm going to leave. I would linger, but one, I'm getting cold and two...two, you can figure out for yourself."

Alexis laughed softly. "If you hang around, we can take care of two."

"No." And he said it with such finality and without the teasing note that had been in his voice that Alexis scooted forward so he could get out of the tub.

The water level dropped taking Alexis out of her warm cocoon. She crossed her arms over her breasts and hugged herself. It wasn't the same.

Dylan grabbed both her bath towels and dried himself as best he could, then tossed them on the floor to help absorb the water.

"Hey. You only left me a hand towel."

"I'll call housekeeping and have them bring you more towels. Run some warm water and stay put." He didn't even look at her.

Alexis didn't know what to think. She watched as he picked up his socks and shoes and the stray objects from his pockets and the sodden blanket, all without saying a word.

"It looks like you're fleeing the scene of a crime," she said at last. Did he feel guilty, was that it?

"You've got thinking to do and I don't want to distract you." He headed for the door, then turned back. "By the way, I do adore you."

And then he was gone.

10

BUT ALEXIS DID NOT RUN any warm water. The after-glow was gone, anyway, and warmth would only make her fuzzy brained. She needed cold, clear sharpness to figure out what the hell had just happened.

Okay, she knew what had happened, she just didn't know why.

Dylan was trying to make a point and it was more than that he was a sexual magician.

Alexis shivered. Being cold wasn't helping her think. She got out of the tub, walked across the cold, wet, floor and put on the terry-cloth robe. With the hand towel, she absorbed enough of the water in her hair to keep drips out of the collar of the robe.

Swabbing the towels and blanket around, she made sure water wasn't leaking into the bedroom.

"Hello?"

"In here." Alexis wasn't at all surprised to find Sunshine standing there with a pile of towels. "I've made a mess." And she wasn't referring only to the water on the floor.

Sunshine giggled and handed her a towel. "So how was your bath?"

"Very...relaxing."

"And?"

"And what?"

"And Dylan."

Alexis shot her a look. "What about him?"

"Well, he was in here with you."

"How do you know?"

Sunshine pointed. "There's a trail of wet footprints that leads from his room to your bathroom."

Of course. "I don't know," Alexis admitted as she helped Sunshine mop up the floor. "I can't figure out what Dylan is doing."

Sunshine straightened. "Oh. And here I thought he'd be a good lover. Guess I can't pick 'em like I used to."

"Oh, he probably is." Definitely, but there are only so many things you share with a friendly maid.

"You didn't…" Sunshine raised her eyebrows.

"I'm engaged to Vincent, but I…did behave inappropriately."

"Oh, honey, if I got a dollar for every time I behaved inappropriately—oh, wait, I did."

Alexis gave an unwilling chuckle. "I don't know what to do. Vincent is the smart choice—"

"But you love Dylan. And he loves you. And he's got money, too. *And* he's younger. Which wouldn't be good if all you wanted to do was inherit but, hey, Dylan is somebody you'd want around."

Alexis didn't ask how she knew all this. "Maybe I'd give up a lot if I married Dylan. Not that he's asked."

"Is this about those marriage papers?"

Alexis nodded.

"I don't see what the problem is. Just have one of those agreements with Dylan. How simple is that?"

Alexis wasn't going to explain how opposed to a pre-nup Dylan was. "It just wouldn't work."

Sunshine pulled down the covers of the bed and to Alexis, nothing looked more inviting. She crawled in, damp robe and all.

"You know what?" Sunshine tucked her in. "If I were you, I'd find out a way to make it work."

WAS SUNSHINE THE ONLY ONE who saw how simple all this could be? Honestly.

Sunshine went to Dylan's room where she found the scratched-up copy of the wedding papers—and resisted dropping in on Dylan in his bath, which had to be worth at least one gold star and quite possibly two—and took them with her.

With all these high-priced lawyers around—even more high-priced than the Countess in her prime—it was going to be little Sunshine, who never even went to secondary school, who was going to show them how to make this work.

Sunshine took the papers to the attic room where she wore herself out manipulating a pen, but when she finished, she'd inserted Dylan's name for Vincent's and even made a few changes that ought to make Alexis happy.

She went to show Alexis, but Alexis was asleep, so she left the papers in Dylan's room where he could find them.

There. She looked heavenward. "Save me a seat at the Picnic, Belle. I'm on my way."

ALEXIS'S CELL PHONE RANG in its charger the next morning. *Early* the next morning.

"Hullo?" Her voice was raspy.

"Hey! It's a great day to get married."

Vincent. She groaned. Unfortunately, he heard her. Fortunately, he misinterpreted the reason for her groan. "Now, now. It could be worse. The good news is that I finished early and I flew back on this bright sunny morning. I slept better than I've slept in days and I'm rarin' to go, if you take my meaning."

Oh, God. She took his meaning all too well. "That's great!" It should be great. And it would be great.

So why didn't she feel great?

Did she really have to ask herself?

"But the bad news is that you're snowed in. Some kind of freak storm. But not to worry. We've hired extra highway workers to start clearing things from this end and the inn is working from their end and with this beautiful sunny day, we'll get a path cleared by this afternoon."

He'd had way too much coffee. "I hope so. My mom is stuck in Denver."

"And one more thing." Vincent's voice had changed, which meant that the one more thing was important. "I'm here at Margaret's hotel. What's all this about you not signing the pre-nup?"

"No big deal." Why was she acting as though everything was fine? Well, because this was about her future and not some touchy-feely session in a bathtub with Dylan, she told herself firmly. Just talking with Vincent had made her see that. He was his old self. The man who had inspired her and driven her to achieve more than she thought she was capable of.

She'd been right to agree to marry him. It was the smart choice.

"There were a couple of funkily worded clauses that we straightened out. Margaret was making clean copies for us to sign."

"I've spoken to Dylan this morning about those 'funkily worded clauses' and he's agreed to a conference call. He should be in your room in a few minutes. Margaret will be with me here. Call us back when he gets there."

A few minutes? She wasn't dressed. Her hair. Alexis's hand stole hesitantly upward at the same time she turned to the mirror over the desk.

Ack! Falling asleep with wet shaggy haircuts was never a good fashion idea.

Alexis threw on some clothes and dunked her head in the sink. She'd just wrapped a towel around it—and appreciated the fact that Sunshine had cleared away the sodden mess while Alexis had apparently conked out—when there was a knock on the door.

Dylan, of course, looking as tousled as she. "Do we have business to transact?"

Alexis looked into his eyes, surprised to find them blank for the first time ever. She couldn't get a clue as to how he was feeling. And last night, the entire time in the bathtub, she hadn't been able to see his eyes, either.

"Vincent wants a conference call about the changes," she said.

"Do we need to have a conference call?"

He was asking if she was still going through with the wedding.

"Do we?" she countered.

"Your decision."

They stood in the doorway just staring at each other, with Alexis trying to read Dylan's emotionally blank eyes, until the phone rang.

"Is he there?" Vincent's voice boomed in her ear.

"Just arrived," she answered, still watching Dylan. She gestured with her head. "There's an extension on the writing desk."

Watching her, he crossed the room and paused, his hand on the phone. At her nod, he picked it up.

"Greene here."

"And now we are four." Vincent cleared his throat and launched into the sticking point. "This clause that you have changed was written precisely the way I wanted it written."

"So you intend for Alexis to bear the cost of any 'lack of marital considerations'?" Margaret asked.

"I think that's only fair." Vincent laughed his power laugh. Alexis had heard it too often to mistake it for humor. "Alexis can't expect everything to go her way. And I know that if she gives this marriage as much of her energy as she does her cases, I won't have to invoke this clause."

"It's a disgusting clause," Alexis broke in.

"It's costing me a great deal to make you my wife. I need some guarantees."

Her words to Dylan.

"Then we will have to define 'marital considerations,'" Margaret said.

"I've never been married. I won't know what I consider lacking until I miss it," Vincent said.

"Then some general guidelines," Margaret insisted.

Dylan said nothing, but he turned away and stared at the view of the mountains.

Vincent and Margaret continued to argue back and forth. Margaret was holding her own, even though Vincent could be a bully.

Alexis was about ready to tell Margaret to back off, when she stopped. Two days ago, she would have signed the thing. Now, after meeting Dylan again, she couldn't. She was glad there was a horribly written clause in the contract because it gave her an excuse to refuse to sign.

So Dylan wanted a leap of faith? A gesture? A commitment? Even after she'd made one all those years ago and had been rejected?

Okay. She'd make one. Because she was an idiot. Because she'd learned nothing in seven years.

Alexis had just about had it with all men. She picked up a bed pillow and flung it across the room where it plopped against Dylan's back. If she was going to make a grand gesture, she wanted to see his face while she made it.

DYLAN HAD BEEN STARING at the mountains while everything within him screamed for him to tell Alexis to dump Vincent and marry him. With Alexis and him, the timing was always wrong.

Clearly, she didn't get last night. He'd given her pleasure though he'd held himself in reserve. He'd wanted her to realize how much deeper and more satisfying lovemaking—and marriage—could be when both parties had invested all of themselves.

He couldn't offer her the financial and career guarantees she clearly wanted, but he could offer her a deep, lasting love.

Hadn't it already lasted seven years?

The irony wasn't lost on him. For years, he'd been counseling clients to think with their heads and now he was making the decision of his life with his heart. Right now, his heart wanted Alexis and it was killing him.

Just then, he felt a pillow hit him in the back. Alexis probably thought he wasn't paying attention.

Oh, he was. But was she?

He turned back around and let her see all the longing and all the pain he was feeling. Couldn't she see what was important? Couldn't she believe that they'd work out whatever problems they'd encounter?

Couldn't she see what an absolute jerk Vincent was being?

So Dylan stared at her, with her unmade-up face and her wild damp hair and thought that after today, his life would forever be poorer.

Then she pointed to him and to herself and moved her fingers in the universal gesture for "talk."

He raised his eyebrows. She wanted to talk?

She pointed to the telephone and made a slashing gesture across her neck.

"Alexis, sweetie," came Vincent's voice, "don't make this personal. This is just business."

"Actually, Vincent, I take marriage personally. It's a quirk of mine." She glared at Dylan.

"Fine. But the contract will stand as is. Take it or leave it."

"In that case," she looked straight at Dylan, "I'm leaving it."

She'd turned him down. Alexis had refused to sign the pre-nup with Vincent. That was enough for Dylan. He hung up the phone but he heard Vincent's shouting all the way across the room as Alexis pulled her receiver away from her ear.

Slowly, his heart pounding, he crossed the room, never breaking eye contact.

And speaking of eyes, Alexis's were huge. He knew that Vincent and Margaret would try to get her to change her mind.

Dylan was after her heart. He stood in front of her, took her hand and placed it over his own pounding heart.

Alexis swallowed hard, then took his hand and placed it over her heart, which was pounding as hard as his.

"I'm sorry, Vincent, but I can't accept the terms of the contract. It was a good idea, but the execution was flawed. I'll tell my family and you can tell yours. I know that you'll want to get back to Houston, but I'm going to stay on here as planned for the next week." She moved the receiver so Dylan could hear.

"Think about this, Alexis. Talk to Margaret. I'll check back with you later today."

He hung up.

"Alexis, we can work this out—"

"You heard him, Margaret. And you also heard me. The wedding is off." She hung up the phone.

"Marry me," Dylan said at once.

"You don't fight fair."

"What's fair about love?"

She shrugged. "Nothing."

"Marry me."

"We have to talk."

"Marry me."

"There are some things I need to know first."

"I love you. Marry me. That should cover it."

"If I agree, then what?"

He smiled. She was still holding back. Shaking his head, he repeated, "Marry me."

Alexis closed her eyes. "I hate this. You know I do."

He did. "Marry me." He thought for a moment, then knelt in front of her, holding her hand. He softened his voice. "Marry me?"

Her eyes flew open. "Oh, Dylan." Her whole expression melted into a "yes."

But he had to hear the word. "Marry me?"

Biting her lip, she nodded and tried to tug him up.

He raised his eyebrows.

"Okay! Yes!" she shouted. "I can't believe I'm saying this, but yes, I'll marry you!"

Dylan had risen to his feet at the first "yes."

It was a good thing they were next to the bed. It was a good thing Alexis wasn't wearing very many clothes. Even more fortunate, they were easily removed.

Dylan wasn't aware of who exactly had done the removing. There was a lot of kissing and a lot of tugging and then a lot of skin—hers.

Dylan had spent years suppressing his emotions in favor of logic and, frankly, he was on sensory overload. His fingers could barely work the snap on his jeans. Finally, he had to stop and just stand there help-lessly while Alexis laughingly did the honors.

Finally, they were both in the bed, and Dylan's na-ked body was pressed against the equally naked length of hers.

He held her for long moments, trying to control himself. Right now, he could enter her and within a couple of strokes, he'd be gone.

Alexis was moving against him so he tried to put some space between them. "Slow down," he breathed, fighting to keep from flipping her on her back and burying himself deep within her.

"No. You've had everything else your way. I'm tired of waiting. I need you now. All of you. No fancy stuff. Just the basics and make it quick."

He liked a woman who took charge. "Oh, I can do quick." He moved on top of her and thrust inside, gasping at the pure pleasure of it. The pure rightness.

But he didn't allow himself to move. He wanted to savor this moment, when Alexis was his once more.

"Dylan!"

And he lost himself in the heat of her, forgetting time and place, but never forgetting her, her scent, her taste and the sounds of passion she made.

He thrust deeply and she wrapped herself around him, holding tight as he thrust a final time and shud-dered. He might have seen stars or he could have been about to pass out from the pleasure of it all. He didn't know. All he did know was that he could stay here forever. He could live like this, with Alexis wrapped around him. They could call room service. They'd never have to leave the bed.

Except...he took his weight on his elbows and cupped her face with his hands. Gently kissing her he gazed into her dark, dark eyes.

"Do you want babies?" he breathed.

"You know I do." She stretched, wearing a pleased, but not satisfied smile. He'd take care of the satisfied part in a minute. "But it won't happen now. I'm taking birth control."

"Then I can begin making love to you again right now?"

"Oh, yes." She pushed until he rolled over. "And this time I'm on top."

Later, Alexis stared up at the ceiling. This wasn't the way she'd planned to spend her wedding morning, but she had absolutely no complaints. She'd tried being logical, but once again had succumbed to the sizzle. And Dylan was quite a sizzler.

But this time, this time would be different. This time, love had proven it could last.

THERE WAS NOTHING LIKE the sound of true love. Sunshine had been dancing up and down the hallway outside Alexis's doorway and now she watched Dylan walk back to his room with the swagger of a satisfied man.

Not that Sunshine had ever doubted Alexis—maybe a moment after the bathtub—but this morning, she had wrung that man dry.

Sunshine wanted to say goodbye to Alexis because she just knew that at any moment, Miss Arlotta and the Judge would call for her. The council was probably meeting right now.

Sunshine hugged herself. That tenth notch in the Bedpost Book was hers. She was as good as at the Eternal Picnic. She could feel the grass beneath her feet. There would be grass in heaven, wouldn't there?

Of course. Otherwise, it wouldn't be heaven.

Sunshine couldn't stand waiting to be called, so she floated up to the attic.

But when she got to the room, instead of finding the council sitting around the old oak dining table, she found Miss Arlotta and Judge Hangen with their heads together.

"Has the council already met?" she asked.

Miss Arlotta heaved a sigh.

"Now wait, before you say anything, I know Alexis was going to marry Vincent, but he wasn't her true love. Dylan is her true love and I got them together and he proposed. A bunch of times. So, they might not have been my original couple, but I should get credit for bringing them together. Shouldn't I?" she finished uncertainly.

"Sunshine, honey, I am sorry to have to tell you, but there is trouble brewing."

ALEXIS WAS HIS. He couldn't believe that Alexis was his. And he was definitely hers. He couldn't believe how incredibly intense—and prolonged—their love-making had been.

It was a good thing he'd set the terms of their relationship before he'd slept with her because when he was in her arms, he'd pretty much agree to anything.

He hoped she'd never find out.

Whistling—and he wasn't a whistler—Dylan popped

back in his room to call room service and arrange for a large, restorative breakfast for two to be delivered to her room.

He also wanted to call his family and let them know that if they wanted to see him get married, they were going to have to hightail it to Colorado. Colorado required no waiting time before issuing a marriage license and Dylan intended to take advantage of it. Besides, Alexis's family was already here. By Monday afternoon—Tuesday at the latest, he and Alexis would be married.

Sure they still had a couple of hurdles—even though Alexis had broken it off with Vincent, the man would not take kindly to finding out she'd married his attorney a day or so later.

But they'd worry about that when the time came.

Dylan sat on his bed and called room service. He added a bottle of champagne, too. It was a champagne-in-the-morning kind of day.

He sat back against the pillows that had seemed so uncomfortable last night and listened to the phone ring at his parents'. They were probably at church and he hated to leave a message. Next, he called his boss at home. There was a forwarding number and as Dylan leaned over to get a pen, he saw the old pre-nup papers. He grinned. Wouldn't be needing those.

But then he saw his name. What? He hung up without writing down the forwarding number. What was this?

As he looked at the changes that had been made—changes that presumed a marriage between one Dylan

Greene and one Alexis O'Hara, he became angrier and angrier.

She had to be kidding. He didn't recognize the big childishly loopy handwriting—it must be Margaret's. So Alexis had discussed this with her attorney. This was what she expected? Dylan figured he'd let her have her pre-nup, but this? She still wanted money every year? And household help? She'd actually spelled out that she wanted a maid? And a nanny? And…pin money? What the heck was pin money?

And jewelry. Alexis felt she needed to spell out his gifts to her.

Dylan was furious. He was so angry he scared himself. How could she do this? He thought she'd agreed to marry him without a pre-nup, but she hadn't.

It must have been delivered last night. After he'd changed clothes, he'd headed to the kitchen to make himself a sandwich and that's when it must have been delivered.

Alexis must have assumed that he'd seen it this morning and agreed. Otherwise, why would he have proposed?

The session in bed this morning had been to clinch the deal.

How could he have been so stupid? So gullible? He knew better.

Forget it. Dylan stormed back to Alexis's room and pounded on the door.

"Wha—"

"I won't stay long." He pushed past and flung the papers at her. "Nice try."

Alexis picked them up. "What's this?" She studied them. "It's the pre-nup but...is this a joke?"

"That's what I want to know. A maid? A nanny? Jewelry? And here I thought love would be enough."

She looked sharply at him. "Where did you get this?"

"On my bedside table."

"You don't seriously believe I wrote this." She thrust the papers back at him. "It's not even my handwriting."

"I don't believe you wrote it—Margaret did."

"That's not her handwriting. It looks as though a middle-school girl wrote it. All it needs is little flowers in place of the dots over the *i's.*"

"Who else would write it and leave it in my room?"

"I don't know..." she trailed off, looking thoughtful. "There is one of the maids who's extremely...gregarious. Maybe she—"

"So you're blaming the maid."

"No. If I had done it, I would have taken the responsibility. But I have to tell you that even though I didn't write this one, I still think having a pre-nup is wise."

"Oh, I get it." He could taste the bitterness he felt. "I see this horrible one, then am supposed to be grateful when you suggest a much more reasonable one. I know that game and it's not going to work."

"Dylan—"

"Getting back together was a mistake. A huge mistake." He turned to leave. He had to get away from her.

"Where are you going? We need to talk about this."

Dylan kept walking. "I don't want to hear anything

you have to say. I'm going to pack and I'll be out of here in half an hour."

"You can't go anywhere because of the snow."

He hated it that she was being so calm and reasonable. "I'm leaving if I have to dig my way out."

"Now, Dylan, be rational. Let's talk about this."

"There's nothing to say. Goodbye, Alexis. Have a good life."

He couldn't bear to look at her anymore.

After packing, Dylan literally walked into a wall of snow, but he pushed his way through to the parking lot with very little trouble. Snow wasn't as hard to get through as he remembered.

His car was covered and drifts were up to the window, but the powdery snow melted wherever he touched it. Very strange snow, but he wasn't going to complain.

The snowblowers were out clearing the entrance drive. Dylan soon reached the end of the cleared area and decided just to see what the car could do. He'd meant what he said. He'd get a shovel and dig his way back to Denver if he had to.

But the car cut through the snow as though it were nothing more than heavy fog.

From the roof, Sunshine, Glory and Desdemoaner watched the little red car.

"Sunshine, his righteous anger is melting your snow."

Sunshine moaned. "I got to do something to stop him."

"More snow?" asked Desdemoaner.

"He's so far out and I'm still tired from yesterday's storm. Can't somebody plant some thoughts in his head for me?"

Glory guffawed. "And risk a black mark? You gotta be kiddin', girl."

"Desi?"

"Nope. I'm not good at that, anyway. I can plant thoughts, but more often than not, they're the wrong ones."

Dejected, Sunshine materialized in Alexis's room. "I'm sorry," she whispered.

Alexis was staring out the window where the tiny red car was all but invisible. "So you were the one who wrote all those silly things."

"They're not silly, but I was only trying to show you that it could be done. I don't understand why he's so mad."

"Because me marrying him without a pre-nup was some sort of test of my love, I guess. And I agreed. But I don't even get credit for it."

"Can't you call him with your phone?"

"Already tried. He turned his off. And you know something? It's probably best. He didn't even listen to me. He believed the most outrageous things and wouldn't even let me speak." She gave Sunshine a wry smile. "The same thing I did to him all those years ago." She sighed. "No matter. It wasn't meant to be. Unfortunately, I don't believe I'll ever love anyone else." She shrugged. "So I'm going to marry Vincent as planned. If he'll still have me."

VINCENT WAS VERY NICE about the whole thing. Maybe even relieved, but Alexis was too miserable to notice. Or care. Bring on the pre-nup. She'd sign it. She'd sign anything.

With the path cleared by Dylan and the highway crew, the delayed guests streamed into the hotel and the wedding was back on schedule.

Or it would be back on schedule if things didn't keep going wrong.

First, there was the missing wedding gown that was found only after Alexis declared she'd get married in her pajamas because she just didn't care. Her mother and sister put it down to bridal nerves.

Then the florist was locked out of her van. Alexis said she didn't need flowers to get married. Actually, she expressed herself much more colorfully and Sunshine, who was causing all the delays, knew that Alexis was just hurt enough and just mad enough to ruin her life by marrying the wrong man and there didn't seem to be any way to stop her.

The right man had about reached the edge of the snow, according to Sunshine's lookouts on the roof. In spite of their earlier refusals, they had tried to help by planting thoughts. In fact, all the girls were on the roof concentrating on making Dylan see sense and come back. Sunshine even told Alexis what they were doing and it didn't make a difference to her.

While all this was going on—and frankly, Alexis was afraid she was going to have to speak to the manager about Sunshine's demented ramblings—Margaret brought by the papers for Alexis to sign.

"You're so lucky," Margaret said as Alexis scanned the pre-nup for any new surprises. "I envy you the opportunity to have a family. I gave up my chance for babies to concentrate on my career and I'll admit this to you—though if you tell anyone I'll deny it—I do have regrets. And now, realistically, it's too late for me to change my mind."

"I'm sorry," Alexis murmured, still reading.

"But it's a hard choice. The girls these days get trapped. This generation of men expect their wives to work *and* raise a family. How did that happen? That wasn't what the women's movement was supposed to be about. But you're lucky. Vincent truly doesn't want you to work. You can be a full-time mother. What luxury."

"I'm grateful that I won't have to spend long hours at a job when I have young children." Alexis still scanned the pre-nup.

"Young or old. He doesn't want you to work ever again."

Alexis had only been partially paying attention to Margaret. "No. The whole point is that when I go back to work, it'll be at a higher level than I am now. The level I'd be if I hadn't taken time off. Vincent can do that since he's a partner. And while I'm at home I'll be helping him the way I do now, but it'll be off the record."

Margaret laughed, which was unexpected enough to make Alexis look up inquiringly.

"You don't seriously think you're going back to work?" her lawyer asked. "Not after leading the kind of life you'll be leading."

"Actually, yes I do."

"Why?"

"Because...I'm good at what I do. I worked hard to get where I am. I'm not giving that up."

"Personally, I think you're nuts. Professionally, I'm obligated to point out that if you do go back to work," Margaret said slowly, "Vincent will invoke the marital-consideration clause."

Alexis stared at her. "Oh, come on."

"I think I understand now why he was so insistent on that clause. I wouldn't put it past him to sue for full custody of any children, either."

Alexis's jaw dropped.

"Alexis, I thought you'd discussed this with him."

"I thought we had, too. I mean...there are lots of women who don't want to work. Why isn't he marrying one of them?"

Margaret gave her a direct look. "I suggest you ask him. And, this is both personal and professional advice, ask him before you say 'I do.'"

THE SNOW PETERED OUT about the time Dylan's anger did. For someone who had preached the virtues of emotional detachment when making decisions, he'd certainly let his feelings have a free rein.

That had been one weird snowstorm. Five miles from the inn and not a flake was to be found.

As traffic headed toward the inn passed him, Dylan drove slower and slower until he finally pulled over to the side of the road to think.

Examining what had happened without the red haze of anger clouding his judgment, Dylan had to admit that sneaking a pre-nup into his room was not Alexis's style. And if she'd done so, she would have admitted it.

If he'd given her a chance. Which he hadn't.

And why hadn't he? Because in spite of years of trying to compensate for it, gullibility still got him sometimes—and he was embarrassed when it did. He'd been raised among salt-of-the-earth people who said what they meant with unembellished directness. They didn't have time for games because they were too busy making a living. As he'd discovered, not everyone was raised the same way. So he'd taught himself to look past the words and seek the true motivations of his clients.

Alexis wanted security. And commitment, as well, he thought. Angering him with that ridiculous pre-nup wouldn't achieve those goals. Therefore, she really hadn't known about those papers. She'd never made a secret of her desire for a pre-nup, but she'd agreed to marry him without one. She would rather have one, but she'd still agreed.

It was everything he'd asked of her. She was everything he wanted.

And she was probably getting ready to marry Vincent right now.

Dylan felt slightly sick to his stomach. How could he have blown it twice with her? What was the matter with him? Maybe she wasn't the one who was afraid to commit—maybe he was. He'd asked a lot of her, but he'd only offered her marriage when he was sure she would say yes.

Dylan didn't like himself very much right now. But he liked Vincent even less.

There was something odd there, now that he thought about it. He knew why Alexis wanted to marry Vincent, buy why did Vincent want to marry Alexis? What was in it for him? Besides Alexis. Not to take anything away from her, but the man had avoided marrying for fifty-four years and suddenly popped the question?

There was something about this that they were all missing.

Something Dylan wanted to find out.

And there was some*one* he needed to apologize to.

Someone who'd probably be really good at make-up sex.

And there was someone who made really good cookies at the inn.

Huh? Where had that thought come from?

He turned the car around and headed back to Maiden Falls.

"GLORY HALLELUJAH, he's a' comin' back!"

"Really? Really?" Sunshine wished Glory would let her look through the spy glass, but it was the one thing Glory had taken with her when she'd died—since she'd been spying out her window with it when the gas fumes had overtaken them.

"Yes. I see that little red automobile coming this a' way."

A cheer went up from the ladies on the roof.

"Thank Got. My head aches viz zee strain." The Countess fanned herself.

"Me, I planted sexy thoughts. We all know with what a man thinks." Mimi laughed and drifted below.

"I went for logic," Rosebud said.

"I concentrated on that cute little cookie he ran out on," Desdemoaner confessed.

Sunshine exhaled. "Thanks everybody. I appreciate this. Now all I have to do is stop the wedding until he gets here!"

ALEXIS STILL HADN'T SIGNED the papers. Vincent had, but she hadn't. And he would demand to see a signed and executed copy before they married.

"Mom, I have to talk with Vincent."

"It's bad luck for him to see you before the wedding," her sister said. "Madison, sweetie, don't eat the flowers. You drop them. Let me show you."

Luck? Alexis wondered what they'd do if Leigh and her mother knew how she'd spent her morning. "It'll be bad luck if I don't talk to him."

"But I haven't finished your hair!" Her mother held her hands over Alexis's head. The tag still dangled from the sleeve of her dress.

Since her mother was going overboard with the curling iron, Alexis didn't think interrupting her was such a bad thing. "It's okay. The headpiece will cover it up."

Alexis wrapped herself in the large terry robe and made her way to Vincent's room.

He was already dressed and making stilted conversation with Bob, her brother-in-law who'd been pressed into duty as best man after Dylan left.

"I need to talk with Vincent," Alexis announced, and Bob made a grateful escape.

"If you're going to confess to your relationship with Dylan, I can put your mind at ease. Although I was aware that you both attended law school together, until recently, I was unaware that you had been anything more than fellow students."

Alexis wasn't going to confess anything. "Other than seeing him at a distance occasionally, I hadn't spoken directly to him since graduation. No, Vincent, what I want to know is why you're marrying me."

"Alexis!" He grasped her by the arms—but held her at a distance. "You're beautiful, smart and successful. Why else would I marry you?"

"There are a lot of women you could have married. Why me? Why now? And, why don't you want me to go back to work?"

"Oh, you'll be able to keep your oar in the water by helping me, just as you always have."

"Vincent." She held his gaze. "Do not patronize me."

He gave a resigned sigh, dropped her arms and sat at the little desk. He loosened his tie. "I have a feeling I won't be needing this." He dropped the tie on the table and looked at her.

She waited.

He made a little face. "I want to slow down. At this point in my career, I shouldn't have to kill myself the way the associates and junior partners do. I should get to pick and choose my cases. Play golf. Take long lunches. Vacation several times a year. But I can't, and you know why?"

She shook her head.

"Because of you. You make me look bad."

"I make you look good!"

"And you spent far too long doing it. I have to work harder than you to stay ahead. I don't want to do that anymore. By marrying you, I remove the problem. Others can work the long hours and not achieve half what you do."

She was stunned, but relieved in a way. "You mentored me."

"And look what I created."

Privately, Alexis thought she had a lot to do with her own success, but decided not to contradict him.

"I don't want to be shown up by my assistant. So when I heard my assistant finally, finally express discontent, I grabbed the opportunity."

"I see." She thought for a minute. "I could cut back—"

"You don't have it in you."

They looked at each other. "You realize I can't marry you," she said.

"I know."

There was another silence. "I'm not going to be able to work for you anymore, am I?"

Vincent gave an elegant shrug. "I would prefer not.

I will, of course, see that you receive a generous settlement and my highest recommendation."

"And if I don't resign?"

Vincent said nothing. He was too experienced.

But Alexis knew what would happen. She'd be reassigned to someone else where she would be buried in tedious, low-profile cases. In a few years, no one would remember her.

"Thank you," Alexis said. "You were an excellent mentor and I appreciate all the opportunities you gave me."

Vincent gave her his magnanimous winner smile. "You're most welcome."

She drew a deep breath. "I'm going to stay on here with my family for a few days."

"I understand. Goodbye, Alexis."

He was already on the phone arranging for an airline ticket back to Houston by the time she made it to the door.

Alexis wandered slowly down the hallway. Oh, this was just great. Just fabulous. She had no fiancé, no lover and no job. So much for thinking with her head. Her heart had never got her into this much trouble.

She was going to have to tell her mother and her sister and the rest of her family that they'd made the trip to Colorado for nothing. Her mother would be thrilled that she hadn't cut the tags off her dress yet.

At least Alexis got to see her niece. And then she stopped. This wasn't for nothing. Her family and closest friends were all here under one roof to see her. To spend time together.

So that's what they'd do. It would set the world's

record for making lemonade out of lemons, but she was going to have one heck of a family reunion party.

DYLAN ARRIVED BACK to find everyone in the ballroom at the wedding dinner. So she'd married him. He actually felt as though he'd sustained a physical blow.

There was always divorce, but he wouldn't ask it of her. Not with the pre-nup she'd signed.

No, Dylan had made a huge mistake and he was going to pay for it for the rest of his life.

But how could Alexis go from his bed to marrying Vincent in just a few hours?

Because he'd run out. He'd messed up big-time. He'd run out on a major client and that client's wife. And he'd forgotten all about being the best man.

His personal life was in ashes and his career was going to take a hit, too, so he wouldn't even be able to bury himself in work.

Well, he was going to have to suck it up, apologize and wish everyone well.

He stood in the ballroom doorway. People were milling around. A piano trio was playing and a few couples were dancing. Everyone looked so darn happy. How could they be happy when he was so miserable?

Dylan searched the room for Alexis. He couldn't find her, or anyone dressed as a bride, for that matter. He didn't see Vincent, either.

Pushing his way into the crowd, he finally saw her talking to a group of people. Even she looked happy.

Suck it up, Dylan. He approached her, noting that

she was wearing a pale gray suit and not a wedding gown.

"Alexis." He touched her arm.

She spun around. "Dylan!"

He couldn't tell if she was glad to see him or not. He drew her away from the others. "I want you to know that I wish you and Vincent the very best. I'm happy for you." He kissed her chastely on the cheek.

She swatted him away. "How could you think I would marry Vincent?"

Dylan blinked. "I saw all these people..."

"In truth, I almost did marry him, but I changed my mind. We had an enlightening chat, where he humiliatingly informed me that he was simply removing the competition, and he's gone back to Houston and I'm throwing a big party for my family."

Dylan had stopped breathing when she said she'd changed her mind. *She hadn't married Vincent.*

"If you aren't married to Vincent, then will you marry me?" He sounded desperate. He *was* desperate.

Alexis gave him a haughty look. "What kind of proposal is that? You took off without even giving me a chance—"

"You mean like the way you did to me?"

"Yeah. Like that."

He swallowed. "So I figure we're even. Now will you marry me?"

"What happened to groveling? No, don't bother. I'm off marriage." She swept a hand through the air. "We can still sleep together, though. Just think how much cheaper it'll be when we break up."

"You're still mad." He should have groveled.

"Actually, I'm happy." She made a grand gesture all around them. "I'm surrounded by friends and family. None of Vincent's could make it, so they're mine. All mine. I'm deliriously happy. But if there's one thing I've learned, it's that love just doesn't last."

"Ours lasted—"

"About three hours and then you took off at the very first misunderstanding. Here I had broken up with Vincent without any idea whether you had marriage in mind and then I agreed to marry you without any guarantees." She turned her head away. "So, no, thanks. Not gonna do the marriage thing."

She meant it and Dylan felt a coldness invade his stomach. He had to convince her. He had to grovel. "Please. I love you. I was wrong. Very, very wrong. I'm an idiot. I was...scared."

She tilted her head and regarded him for a moment. Then she wrapped her arms around him, but shook her head.

"It was me. It was all my fault," he continued. "Am I getting anywhere?"

"Let's just enjoy what we've got while it lasts. You are a good lover."

When had being told he was a good lover become an insult? "What can I say to convince you? I am sorry I misjudged you. I've learned my lesson. I want you in my life."

The girl from the kitchen the other night was suddenly standing right next to them.

"Sunshine!" Alexis turned to Dylan. "It's the prenup culprit in the flesh."

"Yeah, and I could get in a lot of trouble for doing this," she said.

"It's all right," Alexis told her. "I know you meant well."

"I'm not talking about that. I shouldn't be visible in this crowd. I'm risking a spot at the Picnic for you, so you'd better pay attention. Now, you tell this nice man that you'll marry him."

"I beg your pardon!"

"He loves you and you know you love him. You're just being pigheaded out of pride."

"You're right." She looked directly at Dylan. "I do love him and it hurt like hell when he walked out today. I don't want to have to go through that again."

He infused his voice with all the sincerity he possessed. "I'm not going anywhere, Alexis."

"You will when all the fun and sizzle stops."

"Honey, you two were sizzling this morning and that sizzle has lasted for years. It ain't going anywhere, either."

While Dylan appreciated Sunshine's help, the staff at this hotel certainly took their romantic honeymooner reputation seriously. "Thanks, but I can handle my own proposal."

"You've been doing a piss-poor job. Offer her that marriage agreement thing."

Not a bad idea. "Alexis, I—"

"Don't. I'm not holding out for a pre-nup. But if I was, it would say one thing—that you agree that I come first in your life. I want real commitment. Years ago, you had obligations and I can accept that. But if you want me to marry you now, you have to tell me that I'll be your number-one priority. You'll be committed to me."

It was exactly what he wanted. "Absolutely. Draw up the papers and I'll sign." He couldn't say the words fast enough.

"I might just do that." She smiled.

It was the most beautiful smile he'd ever seen. There was *yes* in that smile. He didn't need to hear it. He smiled back.

"Wait," Sunshine said. "I still think you ought to ask for a nanny. Kids can be a real handful. I had seven younger brothers and sisters."

They both stared at her.

"Oh." She looked from one to the other. "You're going to marry him, aren't you?"

Alexis nodded.

"That's great!" She beamed a huge smile, huge even for her. "I'll just...this is so great!" And she disappeared into the crowd.

Alexis laughed. "I guess we'd better get to the microphone and tell everybody that this has turned into an engagement party."

"We're not going to need a microphone." Dylan pulled her close and kissed her. It was an attention-getting kiss and Dylan highly recommended it as a way to announce an engagement.

WHILE ALEXIS AND DYLAN PLANNED their life together, a happy Sunshine was summoned before the Judge, Miss Arlotta and the council.

They were smiling—all of them. Even Flo.

"Well done," Miss Arlotta congratulated her. "With

an extra gold star. You have your ten notches by unanimous vote of the council. But that means we're going to have to say goodbye."

Sunshine trembled with hope. "The Picnic?"

Miss Arlotta nodded.

"Really? Oh, I—" She stopped. Even though she could almost feel that grass between her toes, she looked at the others. "On the roof...the others helped me and, well, I can't go if they have black marks because of it."

Miss Arlotta looked down at her hands. "I'm not certain how much help they actually were." She leveled stern looks at Mimi and the Countess. "But there have been no black marks issued because of it."

Sunshine beamed. "Then that's it? I can go?"

As she spoke, a bright light shone in the ceiling and a golden ladder descended. "Oh! I see Belle! Save me a seat, Belle, I'll be right there!" As Sunshine stepped on the bottom rung of the ladder, she waved to the women who'd been with her for so long. "Goodbye, everybody. I'll miss you!"

There was an answering chorus of goodbyes that faded away.

The light was so bright Sunshine had to close her eyes. And when she opened them, grass was tickling her toes.

If you enjoyed what you just read,
then we've got an offer you can't resist!

Take 2 bestselling
love stories FREE!
Plus get a FREE surprise gift!

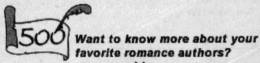

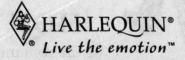

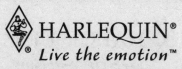

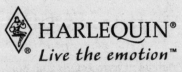